One Night
WITH THE
BILLIONAIRE

One Night

WITH THE

BILLIONAIRE

CASSIE CROSS

Cover design by Mayhem Cover Creations
Interior Design and Formatting by:

E.M.
TIPPETTS
BOOK DESIGNS

www.emtippettsbookdesigns.com

For the latest news on upcoming releases, please visit

CassieCross.com

Chapter 1

"Shut the laptop. Have some fruit."

Kaia Richardson looks up from her computer, which is perched on the sliver of free counter space in the kitchen of the cramped apartment she shares with her roommate, Janine. She rolls her eyes.

"Is there something wrong with wanting to make sure that this presentation goes well? I really need to hang on to these clients. If they like my work, then I'll get more exposure, which means that I'll make more cash, and the first of the month will be a more pleasant experience for both of us."

Janine smiles as she polishes a granny smith apple with the sleeve of her shirt. "We like more cash," she says with a smile, handing the fruit to Kaia.

"We *love* more cash."

Kaia takes a bite of the apple, relishing in the bitter

sweetness against her tongue. She wasn't going to eat anything at all—she usually doesn't when she's nervous—but doing a presentation on an empty stomach probably isn't a good idea.

After she graduated from college four short months ago, Kaia had decided not to pursue full-time employment, opting instead to start her own business as a freelance graphic designer, even though her friends and family thought she was a little crazy to attempt that in today's economic climate. Every time she lands a new client, every time she impresses someone with her portfolio, she proves the people who doubted her wrong.

She likes proving people wrong.

So this presentation has to go well. It *has* to. She isn't willing to leave anything up to chance. If that means polishing each and every one of the logo designs she's presenting to her clients right up until it's time for her to leave for her meeting, then so be it.

"Of course it's going to be perfect," Janine replies. "Those logos are already perfect, and you're going to wear out that laptop if you keep changing them."

Kaia looks up with a crinkled brow. "You have no idea how technology actually works, do you?"

"You know I had a flip phone until recently, and therefore know that my tech savvy is pretty much nonexistent."

Kaia knows that her roommate has a point there. She still has to explain to Janine how text messaging works occasionally. As far as Kaia is concerned, Janine is a twenty-two-year-old in looks, and an eighty-year-old in technological knowledge.

"You really need to stop fussing with that." Janine reaches over the kitchen counter to push Kaia's laptop closed, but Kaia swats her hand away.

"I'm just backing this up to the cloud, in case."

Janine is looking at Kaia like she's speaking in a foreign language, which…well, Kaia supposes that she is.

"It's just a little CYA, my friend."

"CYA?" Janine asks through a yawn.

"Clearly you need more coffee." Kaia reaches for the coffee pot, and brings the spout to the lip of the mug that Janine is holding out toward her. "CYA. Cover your ass."

"Oh. Yeah." She brings her mug to her lips, then pauses to speak. "You think your morning commute is so dangerous that you need a backup?" She takes a sip of her coffee, then smiles at Kaia. "That's one of the reasons I love you so much."

Kaia's commute consists of a short walk to the subway station on the corner of the block, and a single train ride downtown. Still, she says, "Can't be too careful."

Kaia shuts down her laptop and gently closes the lid. She slides it into her computer bag, then dumps her leftover coffee into the sink.

Across the counter, Janine huffs out a little laugh.

"What?"

"It's nothing," she replies with a fond smile.

"It's not nothing. Spill."

"I just think it's funny that you spent so much time on

those draft logos, went to the trouble of backing it up in two places, then put your precious laptop in a bag that looks like that."

Kaia glances down at her threadbare messenger bag. There is a hole in the bottom right, where the canvas on the bottom is dangerously frayed to the point where the corner of the lid is actually exposed.

She needs to replace it, she knows this. Especially given the fact that a lot of her job is based on first impressions, and she definitely wants to give a good one. It's just that the past two months Kaia's had to stretch her money a little further than it wanted to go, and a new messenger bag hasn't been in the budget. Not with rent to pay, and her need to eat at least sometimes.

"Someone would have to slash this thing or hit me *really* hard in order to make my computer fall out." As Kaia slides the strap over her head to rest on her right shoulder, she runs her hand along the bottom of the bag, getting a feel for how weak it really is. Yes, she needs to replace the thing, and soon. "When I lock down this account, I'll buy a new one as a gift for myself, how's that?"

Janine nods, smiling. "It works for me."

Kaia walks over to the floor-length mirror that Janine's mother bought for the two of them, which rests against the wall right next to the front door.

She is wearing her favorite red blouse, one that has a draped front, and is tucked into a black pencil skirt that hugs all of her curves in just the right way. There's a hint of a chill in the late-summer air, so Kaia decided to wear a pair of peep-toe pumps and give her feet one last chance to breathe before fall. She looks down at her red toenails and smiles.

"Should I put my hair up?" Kaia asks Janine, as she runs her fingers through the wavy blonde tresses that cascade down her back.

Janine slides off of the stool she was perched on and pads over until she's standing behind Kaia.

"Nope. You look perfect just the way you are. You're gonna knock 'em dead. Pity about the bag though," she teases with a wink.

Kaia can't even find it in her to be irritated, because Janine isn't wrong.

Janine gives Kaia's shoulder a squeeze, then points at the clock that hangs above the mirror.

"You need to get going or you're gonna be late."

Kaia takes a deep breath and nods. Janine pulls the door open.

"Wish me luck."

"You don't need luck. You're gonna knock 'em dead." Janine's voice carries down the hallway as Kaia makes her way to the stairs.

Thanks to a water main break, Kaia has to take a five-block detour on her way to the subway, and she winds up missing her train. That should be a clue that this morning isn't going to go quite the way she hopes. Still, she holds on to naive optimism that it's just a small wrinkle in what will otherwise be an incredibly smooth and positive day.

Her subway ride proves her wrong.

She's stuck on an overcrowded train, sandwiched between two really tall men, one of whom is transporting a large, pointy metal statue of what looks like it's supposed to be a guitar.

It's not the strangest thing she's seen in New York City by far, but in a minute she'll be wishing it didn't exist.

When the train banks a curve, the handle of the guitar gets caught in the frayed threads that surround the hole on the bottom of Kaia's bag, ripping it clean open. Thankfully, she somehow manages to catch her laptop before it shatters on the floor.

The owner of the deathtrap rolls his eyes at her when Kaia shows him the destruction his sculpture has wrought on her bag. Irritated, she slides her wallet and favorite pen out of one of the side pockets, and puts them in her pocket. She throws the useless scrap of canvas in a trash can as she exits the subway, feeling more than a little dejected.

With her laptop cradled against her chest, Kaia makes her way through the onslaught of morning commuters trying to get to their offices on time. She weaves in and out of the foot traffic, narrowly avoiding any and everyone, because the last thing she wants is for her laptop to become intimately acquainted with the concrete sidewalk.

In order to keep her morning from rapidly spinning out of control, Kaia calms herself by going over her presentation to her clients in her head. She runs through her pitch, point by point. She falls into a nice rhythm that helps calm the panic rising in her chest, which is probably why she's distracted enough to run straight into a very tall, very broad, very *handsome* man.

He clips Kaia's elbow just so, which loosens her grip on her laptop enough to send it crashing to the ground.

Her reflexes aren't fast enough to stop it.

Kaia feels like she's having an out-of-body experience as she watches her computer fall. She stares in horror as it bounces off of the concrete. The casing breaks off in a jagged square, sending part of it flying off, tethered only by some colored wires that are tied to the motherboard or some other internal component that Kaia has no idea how to fix.

Luckily the man she ran into has quick reflexes, and he reaches down and picks up the busted machine off of the sidewalk. The broken piece dangles pathetically as this man cups her elbow and pulls her away from the crowded sidewalk.

"Oh my god," Kaia says, as tears sting her eyes.

"I'm so sorry." The man holds tightly to her computer as he watches Kaia intently.

"Oh my god. Oh my god." This is the only sentiment that Kaia is cable of at the moment. It's all she's thinking. She can't afford a decent bag to carry the thing in; she definitely can't afford to replace it.

"You should sit down," the man says in a very soft, smooth voice, one that somehow manages to make a shiver crawl up her spine even amidst the chaos. He gently presses his palm against the small of her back, where she can feel the heat of his hand through her blouse.

Kaia lowers herself onto the bench, and the man crouches down in front of her. She takes a deep breath and finally manages to get a good look at the guy.

He is *gorgeous*. Wow. Thick dark hair, light brown eyes, and full pink lips that are turned up into a barely there smile. Kaia's heartbeat picks up, leaving her breathless.

"I apologize for my carelessness," the man says, looking up into her eyes. "I'll replace this."

"I should've been paying more attention," Kaia explains, looking down at her hands. "I have a big presentation this morning, and I absolutely need to retain these clients. My bag broke earlier, and I managed to save my laptop from crashing onto the floor on the subway. Guess I'm only allowed one save a day."

After a few beats of silence, she looks up. The man is watching her in a way that makes her want to explain herself.

"Sorry, I'm rambling."

"I like it."

He gives Kaia a smile that makes her knees weak, and she bites her lip to keep herself from smiling as a blush rises to her cheeks.

"I'll just take this," Kaia says, reaching out for her laptop.

As much as she likes being in this man's proximity, she figures it's best to get out of here before she does or says something stupid.

"Absolutely not. I told you I would replace it."

Kaia shakes her head. "It's my fault for carrying it around without a bag."

The man stands, tucks Kaia's busted laptop under his arm, and holds out his hand.

"Come on," he says, helping Kaia up. His touch makes her skin tingle. "You said you have a big presentation this morning. How much time do you have?"

Kaia looks down at her watch. "Forty five minutes or so."

"Plenty of time." He pulls out his phone and starts making arrangements with someone who clearly knows about computers. When he hangs up, he starts walking toward the door of the office building they're standing outside of. "Are you coming?"

"You want me to just follow you inside?"

He grins at her, and that look is like a weapon. "That's the idea, yes."

"How do I know there's not some kind of evil operation in there, and this is a trick?"

He laughs this time, and that's even deadlier.

"Is there something about me that screams evil?"

He's flirting with her, and it unleashes an army of butterflies in Kaia's stomach.

"Not sure yet. The most evil people are the ones who

look…" She has to stop herself from saying something ridiculous.

"Who look what?"

She shrugs, and takes a chance. "Like you do."

The smile melts away, and he stands there looking at Kaia like…like he wants to *devour* her.

She's not all that surprised to find that she wants to be devoured by him.

"Not evil," he says, after licking his lips. "I want you to ace this presentation."

Kaia walks toward him, she can't resist. "Why's that?"

"So I can take you out to celebrate."

Warmth and excitement spreads through her chest.

"Okay."

"What's your name?"

"Kaia," she replies. "And yours?"

"Jason."

Kaia bites her lip, and smiles at the ground.

"Come inside, Kaia," he replies with a knowing grin. "Please."

Kaia walks through the door, and into the building's lobby. She gets the feeling she'll do anything he asks.

Chapter 2

This isn't how Jason Turner usually meets women. At a bar, at a party, sure. On the sidewalk out in front of his building, when he wasn't even looking?

Never.

He has to admit that this run-in is the most pleasant of surprises.

He follows Kaia into the lobby, and a security guard is waiting at the executive elevator, where the doors are already open.

"Good morning, Mister Turner," he says with a smile. He looks at Kaia and tips his hat. "Good morning, Ma'am."

Usually stoic but polite, Jason can't help but return the man's grin. It's been a pretty good morning so far.

"Morning."

Usually the guard would accompany him upstairs, but

Jason gives him a look that lets him know he can stay put. The guard understands. Jason tries not to think about the implication of that look, about what the guard thinks is going to go on in this elevator, given Jason's reputation.

Still gripping Kaia's computer, Jason takes some time to look at her. She's standing relatively close to him, her hands clasped behind her back.

She's beautiful. Gorgeous. Jason has difficulty taking his eyes off of her. Long, wavy blonde hair falls over her shoulders. Her red blouse sets off her light eyes, and the outfit she chose to wear today shows off every single one of her luscious curves.

Kaia is intently looking at the elevator doors. She seems nervous, which Jason finds incredibly charming. It's cute how flustered she seems to be by him. He wants to kiss that shy smile off of her lips, wants to slide his hand down the neck of her blouse to see how far down her blush goes.

"If you don't mind me asking," he begins, wanting to bridge the silence during the long ride. "What is it that you do, Kaia?"

She looks up, her eyelashes fanning over her lids.

"I'm a graphic designer," she replies.

"Which company do you work for?"

"The company of me, myself, and I." She straightens up when she relays that information, standing tall and clasping her hands in front of her. Judging by the defiant look in her eye, Jason realizes that she must've encountered a lot of opposition to that idea, and she's just daring him to doubt her.

Little does she know, that confidence? It turns him on.

Jason holds up her laptop. "This is an especially egregious error, then."

"How so?"

"This is your business," he says. "Your lifeline. You can't be successful without your lifeline."

She gives him a soft smile. "That is very true. Somehow I doubt your lifeline involves a single laptop, though."

"It doesn't," he agrees. "I'm sure at some point yours won't either. Are you just starting out?"

Kaia nods. "Yes. When I graduated from college, all my friends were lining-up these entry level jobs, and don't get me wrong, I think security is important. I just knew that if I started out in the corporate world, I'd probably never leave it, and I didn't want to live the rest of my life working for someone else. It's fanciful, I know."

Jason shakes his head. "Not fanciful. Smart. You're gaining a lot of experience all at once, and whether this venture works out or not, that experience will go with you for whatever you do next."

Jason has years of experience of reading people, and he's positive by the proud look Kaia gives him that he's just repeated back to her an argument she's used with her friends and family.

"I think so, too. If you don't mind me asking," she says, reaching up and tucking a strand of silken hair behind her ear, "what is it that you do?"

"I own an investment firm."

"And you own this building."

He nods. "I do. How did you know that?"

"I didn't, until you just said it. But peons don't have private elevators, so it wasn't a huge leap."

She's teasing him, and god help him, he likes it.

Jason is a serious man, focused and intent on handling his business, but he's no stranger to pleasure. He takes it as he finds it, from a one night stand with a woman he meets in a bar, or a quickie in a coat closet with a hot cocktail waitress at a party. They are flings that never last more than a single night, just the way he likes them.

Then, he's usually the one teasing. He's enjoying the tables being turned.

"Do you enjoy your job?" she asks, which is, quite honestly, the very last question Jason expects.

He has to think for a moment, and purses his lips. Kaia watches him intently, her eyes alight.

"I enjoy being the boss," he says heavily, watching the way her chest rises just before her breath catches. "I like being in control, making sure things go my way. Whether it's here or somewhere else, I think I would enjoy whatever I did as long as my name was on the door and at the end of the day I could make sure things go my way."

Kaia bites her lip and backs up against the wall, a movement that makes her breasts stick out. For a split second, Jason considers reaching out and pressing the emergency stop, so he can find out what Kaia's lips taste like, and feel the velvet of her tongue against his.

But, as Jason gets older, he begins to appreciate delayed gratification. It would be sweet to kiss her now, but even sweeter to do it later, after he's let his imagination run away with him a few times. Imagined the way her breath will feel against his mouth.

He can wait. He's formulating a plan.

Too soon, the elevator reaches his floor, and he steps forward, holding his arm out to keep the doors from shutting while Kaia exits.

"Wow," she breathes, as she looks around the lobby.

Jason has to fight a smile, even though he's pretty sure he wasn't supposed to hear that.

He leads her through a maze of cubicles, ignoring the curious stares of his employees.

When they reach Jason's office, he smiles at his assistant, Ellie, and offers her a pleasant good morning.

"Good morning, Mister Turner," she replies. She hands him a small stack of papers—contracts he needs to sign, he's sure—and gives Kaia a friendly greeting.

Kaia smiles in return.

"Call Clark, please," he instructs Ellie. "Tell him we're here. He knows what this is about."

Ellie nods as she picks up her receiver. Even though Jason can tell she's curious about what's going on and why there's a woman she's never met standing in their office, she doesn't question him, which is one of the reasons he's kept her on for so long, and why he makes sure that her holiday bonus is a generous one.

"After you," Jason says, his hand hovering near the small of Kaia's back.

He watches her intently as she steps into his office. She's immediately drawn to the floor-to-ceiling windows, which offer a gorgeous view of the city's skyline.

"Wow," she replies, looking down with a furrowed brow.

"What is it?"

She shrugs slightly, then turns a small smile on Jason. "I don't think I've ever been up this high in the city before. I knew it was gorgeous, but seeing it is something else."

Jason grins. He understands the feeling.

Kaia turns toward him, looking apprehensive. "Is it okay if I take a picture?"

A warmth spreads in his chest at the fact that she wants to do that, that she'd even ask if she could. He nods, thinking that he could never tell her no.

"Sure. Would you like something to drink?" he asks as she slides her phone out of her skirt pocket.

"No thank you. I'm too nervous."

He can't help but watch her as she frames the picture perfectly on her phone, the corners of her mouth turning up in muted amazement.

She bites her lip as she slips her phone back into her pocket. "I'm nervous about the presentation, by the way. Not nervous about being here with you."

He can tell she wants to say something else, probably to clarify another statement, but there's a soft knock on the door that gets their attention.

"Clark," Jason says warmly. "Come in."

The head of his IT department walks into his office with a loaner laptop under his arm. Rich and powerful as he is, Jason isn't a miracle worker, and this is his best option on such short notice.

"Clark, this is Kaia," he says, as Clark reaches out and shakes her hand.

"Nice to meet you," Clark says.

Kaia replies with, "Likewise."

"Kaia and I ran into each other this morning," Jason explains, holding out her shattered laptop toward Clark. "As you can see, it didn't end well for one of us."

Clark's eyes go wide. "Not sure there's any fixing that."

Kaia grumbles a little, and the only reason Jason manages to resist a smile is because he knows that she's on edge.

"That's where this comes in." Jason points to the laptop Clark has cradled under his arm. "She has a very important presentation this morning. This will get her through it?"

"Yes, Sir." Clark explains, as he flips open the laptop's lid. "This will more than do the job. Getting the presentation off of that mangled hard drive will be an issue, though."

"I have a copy of it saved on the cloud."

Clark's eyes light up. "Oh, well...great. That should be easy. This one's already connected to our secure wifi, so all you need to do is download it. I can do that for you, of course," Clark replies, shooting a quick look at his boss.

"I can do it." Kaia tilts her head at the laptop. "May I?"

Clark hands it over. "Absolutely. Do you need any help, or..."

"I think I've got it," she replies. She walks over to a chair that sits in the corner of his office, and lowers herself onto it. Jason hears her tapping away at the keys for a few seconds, before her eyes light up. "Yep. Got it. Thank you, Clark."

"My pleasure. Anything else I can do for you, Mister Turner?"

Jason nods. "I'm going to send you an email with a project I need you to complete for me. Urgent."

Clark presses his lips together before he says, "Absolutely."

"I'll give you all the details, but I want you to contact me if you have any questions at all."

"Absolutely."

Kaia relaxes back into the chair, after, Jason assumes, she has her presentation loaded up onto the loaner.

"Thank you, Clark."

The IT guy blushes, giving her a smile and a wave as he heads out the door.

"And thank *you*," Kaia says to Jason, with a flirty little smile.

"Me?" Jason teases, as he leans back against his desk, crossing his legs in front of him.

Kaia stands, and carefully tucks the laptop under her arm.

"*You*," she says, walking closer to Jason in what almost seems like a saunter. She comes to a stop and bites her lip, and Jason feels his cock harden in his pants.

He wants this woman. *Badly.*

"But what about your laptop? I ruined it," Jason says, his voice low.

"It died an honorable death, I think," she says, taking a step closer.

Jason has a great view of her cleavage from here. He wants to lick the tops of her breasts, wants to taste the sweet warmth of her skin.

Later, he knows he will, and the thought thrills him.

"Mister Turner," his assistant calls over the intercom, breaking up the tension in the air. "Mister Avery is here for his appointment."

Shit.

Jason looks at his watch. It's just as well, Kaia's going to be cutting it close for her meeting as it is, and his plans for later all hinge on it going well.

"I should be going anyway," Kaia explains. "How should I return this to you?"

"How about you bring it by at seven? Then we can go somewhere and celebrate your successful pitch."

Kaia's face lights up with a gorgeous smile.

"Dinner?"

With a wry smile, Jason nods. "And dessert."

Kaia purses her lips together, then looks down at the floor

as a blush spreads up her neck.

"I'd like that. A lot."

"I'll leave your name with the security guard at the desk, so you can come right up."

Kaia nods. To Jason's utter surprise, she pushes herself up on her tiptoes and presses her lips to his cheek. Jason turns his head, and breathes in the soft floral smell of her perfume. It takes everything in him not to hold her close and say to hell with the day, and spend his hours wrapped up in her.

"I'll see you later," Kaia says, when she pulls away too soon.

"Looking forward to it."

She turns and gives him a soft smile that hides a world of trouble. "Me too."

"Knock 'em dead."

She gives the laptop a little shake. "Thanks for this."

"Anytime." He means that. And if he has his way, she's going to be thanking him for a lot more this evening. Loudly, and often.

Chapter 3

"At least that shitty computer bag was good for something," Janine says. She's sitting on the edge of Kaia's bed, cradling a glass of wine between her fingers.

Kaia shoots her a look. She has just spent the past 15 minutes explaining the events of her surreal morning to her roommate, and *that's* what she chooses to pick up on?

"It worked out well, but what if it hadn't?"

"You would've thought of something, because you're you and you're brilliant." Janine brings her glass to her lips and takes a long sip. "Can't we just focus on the positives here? Because that's literally all there are. You were typically clumsy and ran into a gorgeous guy. Your computer broke, but he insisted on replacing it for you. He could've ended it then, but wants to take you out to dinner to celebrate the pitch that you did, in fact, ace the hell out of."

When Janine puts it like that, despite the shitty beginning, Kaia has had quite a remarkable day.

"I did ace the hell out of it, didn't I?" Kaia steps out of her closet, the evening's dress draped over her shoulders, but unzipped in the back.

She walks over to her night stand and picks up her near-empty glass of wine, then walks over and taps it against Janine's.

"To retaining clients," Kaia says, over the soft clink of their glasses.

"To making rent," she replies with a smile. "And to hot men breaking our laptops."

Kaia raises a brow. "Hoping for something?"

"If tonight goes well, absolutely. I'm going to walk around downtown with some kind of electronic in my arms, praying for the best. Although," she continues with a playful frown, "with my luck, I'll probably get robbed or something."

Kaia laughs, even though she knows that Janine is probably right. She's lucky things turned out for her the way that they did, really. And she's not really sure how to respond to her friend's joke, so she just gives herself a once-over in the mirror hanging behind her bedroom door.

She's wearing a black halter-top with a flared skirt, and her highest, strappiest heels.

"Is this a good dress?" she asks.

"It's a great dress. Appropriate for dinner, and the loose skirt with easy access for dessert."

Kaia laughs, and smiles at Janine over her shoulder. "I like the way you think."

Janine stands, and walks behind Kaia, gently zipping up the back of her dress, which now, instead of hanging loosely, hugs her curves in all the right places.

"Should I put my hair up?"

Janine tilts her head to the side, considering it. "Nah, it's kind of wild and wavy and sexy. It's the way you were wearing it this morning, and obviously this guy liked it enough to want to see more. I say leave it, as long as you like it."

Kaia loves it. She feels sexy, and knows she looks good. It's a rare combination for her, so she holds onto it when she can.

"Nervous?" Janine asks.

Is she nervous? She's about to go meet and have dinner, then *dessert* with a gorgeous, seemingly generous man who already pretty much told her he wants to have sex with her. She definitely wants to have sex with him.

"An anticipatory kind of nervous. I just wanna...get to it." She wonders briefly if it's okay to admit that.

Janine laughs. "I don't blame you. Should we have some kind of emergency exit strategy in place? Just in case things go south?"

"I'm kind of hoping things go south," Kaia teases, as Janine picks up a pillow and pretends like she's going to launch it in Kaia's direction.

"If you didn't look so hot, I'd beat your ass with this fluffy thing," she says, before tossing the pillow back on the bed. "If things don't go the way you're hoping, then text me with some kind of a code so I'll know I need to call you and make up some reason for you to leave."

Kaia's stomach plummets at the suggestion that such a thing could happen. She doesn't even want to put that possibility out into the universe.

"I think we can skip it this time."

Janine gives her a skeptical look. "You're trying to tell me that the woman who was saved by a last-minute posting to the cloud after some gorgeous man turned her computer into a pile of plastic and wires is going to leave this apartment tonight without a safety net?"

Janine's got her there.

"Good point. Things don't work out, I'll text you with nine-one-one, and then you can call me and make up some plausible and yet not real excuse. I don't want to get jinxed or something, so...no killing off my grandmother."

Janine furrows her brows. "Your grandmother's already dead."

Good point. "Okay, just...no one dies, they just get sick, okay? Or maybe a friend had a bad breakup, or...whatever, just come up with something good. But I'm positive I won't need you to rescue me."

"Better safe than sorry," Janine says, as she watches Kaia apply a coat of shiny lip gloss. "Speaking of, I put a whole package of condoms in your clutch."

"You're expecting more than I am," Kaia teases, although...

it would be nice if things went *that* well.

Janine shrugs. "Aim high."

Kaia wiggles her brows suggestively as she slides her gloss and a mirror into her clutch.

"Here's hoping I don't have to tell him that."

Chapter 4

Jason Turner has lived his share of long days; people don't get to be at his level without putting in the hard work. Even though he was born with both of his feet firmly planted halfway up on the ladder of success, he still had to do the work that took him the rest of the way up.

Now that he's there, he would never try and convince anyone that his life is difficult. It's not, by any stretch of the imagination. He has more money than he could ever possibly spend, a comfortable home, and he definitely has his choice of women.

Still, some days are an absolute slog to get through, and today has been one of them.

Jason can attribute that to the never-ending meetings he sat through, the pile of contracts he's had to read and sign, or the sheer number of emails he needs to respond to that are steadily piling up in his inbox. Instead, he's going to lay the blame directly at the feet of the problem: Kaia.

No matter how hard he's tried, he hasn't been able to stop thinking about her all day.

As the clock crawls slowly toward 7, all he can think about is the way her body felt against his when she kissed his cheek this morning. The sweet smell of her perfume, the soft touch of her lips, the way her soft breasts pressed against his chest. Thoughts of her are *consuming* him.

Jason isn't the kind of man who has a lot of regrets—he has some, of course, but not many—but he definitely regrets not kissing Kaia right then and there. He's been thinking about it all day, been driven to distraction wondering how it would've felt to turn his head and taste her.

She's due to be here any minute, and despite the fact that he's been looking forward to this all day, he's nowhere near ready. He wanted to be prepared to leave, jacket on and ready to go, so they were that much closer to the end of dinner and the beginning of a long night in bed. Even though he's been preoccupied for hours, this is the first moment he's stopped to take a breather all day.

His jacket is flung over the back of his chair, his shirtsleeves rolled up to his elbows. He knows that most men would go down and meet Kaia in the lobby, but Jason is not most men, and he doesn't want her to get the wrong idea about what this is. It's one night, nothing more, and he's going to make that very clear before they go out, so Kaia can change her mind if she wants to.

As if on cue, Kaia appears at the doorway of his office. She gently knocks.

"Hi," she says softly. "I'm a couple of minutes early, and I decided not to be that girl who hangs around outside just to be punctual."

Jason grins at her before his breath catches in his throat. She looks gorgeous.

Amazing.

Her dress is low-cut, dipping down between her full breasts. The skirt is short and swishy, flaring out from her slender waist. She's wearing high heels with straps that wind their way up her long, long legs, which are tanned and toned. Jason can't wait to explore the silky smoothness of the insides of her thighs with his mouth, wants to know what her legs feel like when they're wrapped around his hips.

"Hi," Jason finally replies. He stands from his chair, and licks his lips as he gives her a long, appreciative look. He's pretty sure he made what he wants from her very clear, but just in case she didn't get the message earlier, he makes sure she gets it this time. He steps out from behind his desk and says, "You're beautiful."

A blush creeps up Kaia's cheeks, and she smiles as she offers him a soft thank you.

"Come in," he says, leaning in and pressing a kiss against her cheek as he quickly closes the door behind her. "I can tell that we're going to be celebrating tonight, like I knew we would be."

"We are. I aced it."

Jason smiles. "I knew you would."

"Thanks to you. And to this, which…well, I guess this is thanks to you, too." Kaia holds out a large bag, and Jason takes it from her. The laptop is inside.

He pins her with an intense look, her eye wide.

"Don't ever give someone else credit for work that you did," he explains. "You came up with the designs, and you gave the presentation. You could've done that regardless of whether I loaned you a laptop. Especially since I was the one who broke it in the first place."

Jason watches her throat constrict as she swallows.

"Okay," she replies, her voice unsteady. She straightens her back, and looks him in the eyes. "I aced it. Because I'm awesome and good at my job."

Laughter surges out of him. "You're damn right. Now," he says, taking a few steps over to the chair that sits in the corner of his office. "This is for you."

Jason picks up the supple handles of the leather bag, and hands it over to Kaia.

"What's this?" she asks with wide, beautiful eyes.

"Your new laptop. And something for you to carry it in, so you don't have a repeat of this morning. The next guy you run into might not be so nice," he teases.

Kaia slides her fingers along the edge of the bag, the slowly slides the zipper back and pulls out the laptop.

"Oh wow," she breathes. "This is so much nicer than mine." She bites her lip as she looks at the machine, then slides it back inside the bag. "I can't accept this."

Jason expected this would happen, and he holds up his hands. "You can, and you will. I firmly believe that when you break something that belongs to someone else, you always replace it with an upgrade."

Kaia gives him a skeptical look. "Aren't you supposed to replace it with exactly what you broke?"

"Some people might. Not me. Besides, an entrepreneur needs the best equipment she can get her hands on."

She nods, her lips curving up into a small smile. "Thank you."

"You're very welcome. Do you feel comfortable giving me your address, so I can have someone drop it off to you?"

Kaia looks at him quizzically.

"You're probably going to be distracted tonight," he says, sliding his fingertips across her shoulder, and watching the goosebumps bloom across her skin. "I don't want you feeling like you have to keep track of it."

After inhaling a shaky breath Kaia replies teasingly, "A gentleman would keep track of it for me."

Jason takes a step forward, right into Kaia's personal space, and he can hear her shaky intake of breath.

"Tonight, I think you'll find out how much of a gentleman I'm *not*."

Her eyes flash up to meet his, wide and bright. Then she

blushes, and looks down at her hands.

"I'm looking forward to that." she tells him softly. "I've actually been looking forward to it all day."

Any restraint he has left in him just…breaks.

Jason leans down and kisses Kaia. He hears the sharp thud of something hitting the floor—probably the sparkly golden clutch she had tucked under her arm—as her hands grip the fabric of his shirt. She tastes strongly of mint; knowing that she actually prepared before coming over makes Jason smile for a moment, even though that makes the kiss a little awkward for a moment.

These short, soft moans escape from the back of Kaia's throat as Jason licks his way into her mouth. Each noise cuts away at his remaining self-restraint, or…what little bit is left of it, anyway.

His hands roam her body, unable to settle on one place for more than a few seconds. His fingertips dance across the bare skin that peeks through the cutout on the back of her dress. He wants more, he *needs* more, and if the noises Kaia's making are any indication, she's right there with him.

Jason turns them and gently guides Kaia back toward his desk. He backs her up against the surface, then lets his hand slip down to her hips and around the lush curve of her ass so he can lift her enough to set her on the desk.

It surprises a yelp out of her, making Jason pull back, his eyes lidded and his breathing heavy.

"Is this okay?"

He barely gets the words out before Kaia is wrapping his tie around her hand and using it as leverage to pull him close enough to kiss.

"It's more than okay," she whispers against his lips. "I've wanted you to do that since this morning."

Jason is surprised, and yet somehow not, thankful that the two of them are both on the same page, at least as far as wanting each other goes.

"Good," he replies between kisses. "I've been wanting to do that since this morning."

A slow, sexy smile curves Kaia's lips, as her tongue flicks out and licks away his taste. The sight of it makes Jason even harder than he already was.

Tonight, this woman just might be the death of him.

"Yeah?" she asks.

Jason hums in affirmation.

"What else have you been wanting to do?"

Jason's mind goes temporarily blank, because the list is too long, and he's not about to get down and dirty with her in his office where they're limited by noise constraints and lack of available surfaces. Sure, he's a sexually talented man, and he could blow her mind even if he only had the floor to work with. But he'd like to luxuriate in her body and blow her mind, and for that? He definitely needs a bed.

Slowly, so *slowly*, he slides his fingertips along her inner thigh, until he reaches the frilly edge of her panties.

She's so *wet* for him already.

"This," he says, voice deep as he shifts his hand between her legs, making her moan. "Definitely this."

Chapter 5

Kaia opens her legs wider to make room for Jason, as he slides his other arm around her waist and gently slides her so she's sitting right at the edge of the desk. Her skin tingles with anticipation. She wants nothing else in this world but to have his hands on her.

Anywhere.

Everywhere.

Jason's fingertips push her underwear to the side, so he has full access to her. With hunger in his eyes, the pad of his thumb slides across her clit, and she lets out a high-pitched whimper, bucking her hips up, needing more pressure.

In response, Jason leans in, kissing his way down her neck. His mouth is so soft, and yet so insistent. Pressing against her, sliding across her skin. He licks and sucks, probably leaving a mark. Kaia doesn't care at all, she wants him to leave behind any reminder of this night, of this moment.

She turns her head toward him, cheek brushing against his soft hair. She breathes in the clean smell of him, which makes something flutter in her chest, makes her *need* him more than she already does.

"More," she whispers, making his hair flutter with her breath. "Please." She shifts her hips, but his thumb is still barely there, lightly stroking, driving her crazy. "I need more."

Jason lifts his head, completely abandoning the work he was doing on her collarbone. His lids are heavy; he looks drugged. Kaia is positive she looks the same way.

"More what? You have to tell me what you want if you expect me to give it to you."

Because he seems intent on teasing her, Jason removes his hand, waiting for further instructions. The thing is, Kaia's mind is completely blank. She just wants *more*, whatever that means to him, whatever will make him get her off.

"Please," she says. "I just want…I need…"

The blissed-out haze on his face disappears when he pins her with an intense look.

"Tell me what you want," Jason replies in a commanding tone that Kaia imagines he uses quite a lot to get his way. She's surprised to find that it ramps up her arousal a thousand percent. He leans forward, and gently tugs her earlobe between his teeth, his lips brushing over the shell of her ear when he growls, "Tell me now."

"I want to come," she says. She's so desperate for it that

she can't even find it in her to be embarrassed about being so forward.

He grins. "Good. I want to make you come. How would you like me to do it?"

Kaia lets out a frustrated groan. "Every way. All the ways. With your tongue, with you inside of me, with your-"

"Kaia."

The demanding way he says her name makes her shiver. He has her full, unwavering attention, and she can tell that he knows it.

"Yes?"

"If you give me the opportunity," he says, sliding his hand across her breast, which is still covered by the fabric of her dress. Her nipple puckers at the sensation. "I'm going to make you come so many times tonight that you'll lose count. I'll do it any way you want me to. But now, right *now*, how do you want it?"

That's an easy enough question for her to answer, and she makes her decision based on proximity.

"Your hand. I want you to use your hand."

Without wasting even a second, he has his hand between her legs. He slips two fingers inside of her, and she plants one hand on the desk to give her some leverage so she doesn't topple right over. Jason curls his fingers up, hitting just the right spot inside of her, and her head drops back as she lets out a soft moan.

"Look at me," Jason says, his voice low and rumbly.

She does. Right now she'll do anything he asks her to. His honey colored eyes are piercing, and she couldn't look away even if she wanted to.

His fingers are moving in and out of her in a rhythm that's driving her crazy. The pad of his thumb rubs her clit as he fucks her with his fingers, driving her higher and higher. She moves her hips to help herself along, and he adjusts what he's doing for her.

They're so in tune it's ridiculous. She's never felt so attracted to someone who's virtually a stranger. If she gave herself time to think about what she's doing with a man she doesn't even know, she'd probably be mortified.

Good thing she's so far gone she's incapable of regret.

He drives her right to the edge, to the point where she's so close to falling she's losing control. Unfortunately for her, Jason somehow anticipates it, and he slows everything down. She's still feeling good, feeling every soft brush against her clit like an electrical current all the way down to her toes.

But it's not enough. Not nearly enough.

Kaia leans up and presses her lips to his, where they meet in a slow, languid kiss. Jason sucks on her tongue, nips at her lip, basically drives her crazy. She loves the feeling of his stubble rasping against her skin, and she realizes that she could kiss him for hours. She could lose *days* to it, it's that good.

Kaia rocks against his hand, wanting whatever it is that he's willing to give her, and wanting it *now*. Jason twists his wrist, moving in a way that gives Kaia something sturdy to grind against.

She reaches out and grips his forearm, not wanting him to move from that spot.

"Is this good?" he asks, pressing his forehead against hers as her breathing picks up. "Fuck, you're wet."

"Y…yes," Kaia stutters. "Don't move. Just…just let me…" She loses her train of thought as she loses control of her hips, pleasure shooting its way through her as she comes with a shout.

Jason's free hand plays with her nipple as he sucks on a spot right below her ear, and she's so weightless, so blissed out that she feels like she could fly.

"Wow," she finally breathes, when she has her wits about her. She pulls back and looks at Jason, who's giving her a sly grin. Kaia doesn't even want to think about how many orgasms he's given women to be as good at it as he is, but she sure is grateful.

"There's more where that came from."

The tone of Jason's voice makes Kaia's heart skip a beat. "I'm looking forward to it. And," she says, reaching down and sliding her palm against his rock-hard cock. "I'd like to repay the favor."

He hums as he leans in for another kiss. "Can't wait. There is one condition, though."

That cuts through the post-orgasmic haze that Kaia's been floating in, and it makes her stomach sink like it's made of lead.

"Okay," she says, drawing out the word expectantly. She's

just hoping that whatever it is doesn't ruin him for her, because the orgasm she just had? She doesn't want it to be her last with this man.

"I don't do relationships. So this thing?" He motions between the two of us. "It's just for tonight. If that's not something you can deal with, then you can go home if you'd like. Or you can accompany me to dinner; that offer is still good."

Kaia considers that. Of all the things Jason could've told her, it's pretty much the least devastating. She's not exactly surprised that someone who looks like he does would want to keep his options open.

She's so drawn to this man that the thought of just one night with him leaves her feeling a little sad. But Kaia tries not to live her life with regrets, and she would regret going home alone tonight.

"What if I want to skip dinner, and get straight to the orgasms?"

Jason lets out a startled laugh. "That can be arranged."

Kaia reaches down between them, and grips his cock through his pants. It's a move that she can tell he wasn't expecting, based on his surprised reaction. He actually growls at her as he leans in and drags her bottom lip between his teeth.

"Arrange it, then."

Jason lifts Kaia off of the desk, then grabs his jacket from his chair.

"Come on," he says, taking her hand and leading her out

the door.

"Where are we going?" She can't take him back to her place, and if he's dead set on one-night stands, he probably doesn't take women back to his.

"I have a room. The hotel isn't far."

The executive elevator is open and waiting for them. When the door closes, Kaia lifts up on her tip toes, and presses her mouth against Jason's.

If she only has one night with him, she's making every second count.

Chapter 6

In an extravagant hotel room not too far from his office, Jason is sitting on the edge of a plush mattress, his fingers fisting into silky soft, high thread count sheets.

Kaia stands in front of him, naked. He tore her dress off somewhere in the foyer, plucked her bra from her gorgeous breasts shortly after, then ripped the delicate lace panties from her hips with little more than a flick of his wrist.

Kaia's hair is wild and wavy, completely undone from Jason's insistent fingers running through the strands. Her lips are swollen from his kisses, and he can see the path of red skin that bloomed in the wake of his mouth as he nipped and licked his way across her chest. Her nipples are taught and pink from his teasing, and he can't wait to get his mouth on them again.

Jason doesn't think he's ever seen anyone look as gorgeous as she does in this moment. He's still fully clothed—seems

Kaia has a lot more restraint than he does—and his cock is aching for her.

"What do you want?" she asks with a sly grin, relishing in giving him a taste of his own medicine.

Jason expected this. He was looking forward to it, actually. He reaches out and caresses Kaia's hip.

"I want to come," he replies.

Unexpectedly, Kaia drops to her knees. He expects her to ask him how he wants it, but she doesn't. She just gets to work on unbuckling his belt.

Jason reclines, resting his elbows on the bed as he watches her in this unguarded moment. He takes the opportunity to notice the different colored blonde flecks in her hair, and the shiny lacquered red coating her fingernails. He imagines that color contrasting with his skin, the way it will look and feel when she's gripping his cock.

Her hair falls forward in a curtain, blocking his view of her face, so Jason reaches forward and pushes it back, draping it across her neck so it falls on the other side of her shoulder.

When Kaia has his pants undone, she shimmies them down just far enough to expose his erection, which is straining beneath the cotton of his boxer briefs. She traces it with her finger, then rubs it with her hand, winding him up.

"Should I touch you?" With a gentle pressure, she caresses him, and his hips buck up for more friction.

"Mmm," Jason hums. He likes that, she can keep doing that.

She lowers her mouth to his groin, tracing the outline of his hard cock with the tip of her tongue. It's immensely erotic, feeling the light tickle and hot breath through the cotton. She moves along his shaft, then there's a little flick of her tongue as it traces the head.

He sits up, startling her, and possesses her mouth with his. It's wet and needy, because he can't wait, and he can't get enough of her.

Jason kisses his way down Kaia's neck, all the way to her breasts. He cups one of them in his hand, rubbing her nipple with the pad of his thumb, as he takes the other one in his mouth, laving his tongue across the pebbled skin. When he tugs it through his teeth, Kaia lets out a soft moan, then bunches the hair at the nape of his neck between her fingers.

That's when Jason completely loses control.

He stands, shedding his pants and his underwear with one quick movement. He's a little clumsy about it, which makes Kaia giggle. A giggle that, in turn, makes Jason want to kiss the sense out of her, so he does just that.

"I want…" he says, before he loses all train of thought. She's gripping his cock, and her thumb is sliding across the wetness at the tip, making him lose his mind.

"That feel good?"

Jason closes his eyes in pleasure, and manages a nod. "Yeah. Feels good. Feels amazing."

Kaia pushes up on her tiptoes, and sucks on a spot right next to Jason's Adam's apple. Somehow her lips on his skin manages to heighten every single sensation.

"I want inside of you," he manages. "I want to be inside of you now."

He can feel the smile that curves her lips, and before he has time to register the absence of her touch, she's wrapping her fingers around the placket of his shirt, and pulling. The buttons give way, one by one.

Panic pushes through the foggy haze in his mind, because he hasn't had time to tell her about his scars, hasn't had time to prepare her for what she's going to see. As handsome as his face is, he never quite gets over the look that flits across women's faces when they see the rest of him isn't so perfect.

He steels himself as Kaia peels back his shirt, letting it fall over his shoulders and off of his arms. The lights are dim in the room, but she'll see, there's no way she won't.

The trepidation or surprise that Jason expects never comes. Instead, Kaia rakes her nails across his abs, making him flex, and a smile crosses her face.

"Your body is *insane.* I don't think I've ever touched muscles like these. Not with my hand, and certainly not with my mouth, which I'm going to be using a lot of tonight, I can tell. I hope you're ready for that."

He's had these brutal scars since he was fifteen years old, long before he'd ever shared his body with a woman. And not once in the years since has someone *not* noticed them. Or, if he dares to let himself imagine this is the case where Kaia is concerned—not *cared.*

"I'm ready." He is. He's more than ready. And there's a lightness in the air that he hasn't felt in years. It makes him giddy. So giddy that he playfully tosses Kaia onto the bed. He pulls a condom out of his pants pocket, then crawls toward her on his hands and knees, like a hunter after his prey.

Chapter 7

Kaia watches Jason as he puts on the condom, his beautiful body on display. Even though he did a lot to hide it, he seemed to be a little anxious about her seeing him. She felt the scars when she was kissing him, could make out the topography of them under his shirt. She knew to expect something, and she could tell by Jason's furrowed brow that he thought he was hideous.

She'd never voice this aloud, but Kaia thought there was an elegance to the way they dotted and swept across his torso. Focusing on the abstract beauty of them was an easy way to distract herself from thinking about what he'd gone through to get them. Jason didn't seem like a person who would like to be pitied, so Kaia absolutely was not going to pity him.

She wanted him inside of her too badly to do that.

Jason plants one hand next to Kaia's head, then leans down

and kisses her. She wraps her legs around his waist, pulling him closer. The tip of his cock brushes against the wetness between her legs, and she bucks her hips, hoping for more.

"Anxious, are we?" Jason teases.

Kaia is breathless. "I've been anxious since I left my apartment."

Jason raises his brow. "Why's that?"

"You know why."

"Say it," he says, that commanding tone in his voice again. All the playfulness that was in his eyes earlier is gone, replaced by this focused intensity. "Tell me what you want me to do to you."

Kaia licks her lips. She's not usually one for dirty talk, but she seems to be willing to do a lot of things she's not used to as far as he's concerned.

"I want you to fuck me. Hard." She also wants it soft and slow, but she's not sure she should ask for that. She figures there's time. Later.

Jason doesn't waste a second. He cradles himself between Kaia's legs, and slides inside, giving her a moment to adjust to the size of him.

"Christ," he says, burying his head in the curve of her neck. "You feel so good." His hips snap into hers as he gets his bearings, then raises his head and looks at her. "So fucking good."

Kaia wraps her arms around Jason's shoulders, hanging on for dear life. She asked for it hard and fast, and that's exactly what he's giving her. Their skin slaps together as they kiss frantically, pleasure coiling up inside of her. She's not going to last long like this, and she doesn't think he is, either. There's too much anticipation in the air, too much want...

"Touch yourself, Kaia."

The sound of her name on his lips as he moves inside of her makes her crazy with want.

"*Do it*," he commands. "Rub your clit *now*."

Kaia slides a hand between their bodies, and does as he asks, sparks thrumming through her veins, igniting every nerve inside of her body.

She bites her lower lip, not wanting to embarrass herself, as her pleasure spikes higher and higher. She's losing the thread, unraveling...

"I want to hear you," he says, voice low and rumbly. "Don't hold back."

She looks up at him, still unsure about doing what he asks for whatever reason, even though she's hurtling toward an orgasm as he pistons inside of her.

She *wants* to yell, she just...

Jason stills, his hand cupping her cheek. "You told me you wanted to make every second of tonight count," he says, chest heaving. "And I won't know how much harder I need to make you come a second time, if I don't have a starting point."

Oh god. The promise of *more* leaves her breathless.

"Give me a starting point," he says, as he starts steadily rocking into her. "Let me hear you."

Kaia plants her feet on the bed, and uses the mattress as leverage, riding herself against him, her clit rubbing against the ridge of his cock in the perfect way.

"Make me scream, then," she challenges.

With his hands fisted in the sheets, and sweat beading across his brows, Jason does just that.

He follows her seconds later.

Early that morning, Kaia has a delicious ache between her legs. Jason had made good on his promise, making her come harder and scream louder their second go-round, and then again on their third. She came again with his face between her thighs, then gave Jason what he described as, "the best fucking blow job of my life."

All-in-all, not a bad way to spend the evening. Especially not when she opens her eyes with his arms wrapped around her, his chest a solid wall of muscle at her back.

She finds herself wanting to ask about his scars, wanting to find out things about him that she can take with her when she goes. She knew that wanting more was a risk she was taking when she agreed to this whole thing, she just didn't take the time to consider that she'd actually *want* more.

Kaia shakes her head, banishing those thoughts. Nothing good can come of them.

"Can't sleep?"

Jason's voice is low and rumbly, but it doesn't startle her.

"You wore me out," she says with a soft laugh, and she's not sure she's imagining Jason's arms pulling her closer. "But I wasn't sure if sleeping was part of the whole one-night-only bargain."

Truthfully, she'd planned on being gone when he woke up. She doesn't want to make this any more difficult or weird than it already will be.

Jason presses a kiss to the back of her neck.

"Sleeping is allowed. I…"

His voice falls off, because he is clearly rethinking whatever it is he was going to say. Kaia's too curious to let it drop, though.

"You what?"

"Nothing," he replies. "It's probably better if I don't say it."

Kaia turns in his arms, until she's facing him. She presses a kiss to his lips, because she just has this one chance, and the clock is ticking, and she doesn't want to waste a single second.

"Well, that did absolutely nothing to quell my curiosity."

Jason laughs. "I have an early flight," he explains. "I have a meeting in San Francisco. But if I didn't, I would've liked to take you to breakfast."

There's a fluttering under Kaia's diaphragm when she hears those words. But they don't mean anything, not really. They're designed to make her think that a door is open, when it's really shut.

"Yeah." Kaia tilts her head down, unable to look Jason in the eye. "It would've been better if you hadn't said that."

Because she wants it. She wants breakfast and more, and

she knows, she *knows* she can't have it. Maybe that's why she wants it so badly, because it's just out of reach.

She looks at the clock. It's quarter to six; might as well make a break for it now. This isn't going to get any easier.

Kaia rolls to her side, only to be caged in by Jason's strong arms.

"Where are you going?" he asks. His brows are furrowed in genuine confusion.

"I think I should probably go."

"No, I…" He lets her go, then rolls over on his back, sliding his fingers through his hair as he stares up at the ceiling. "I knew I should've kept my mouth shut."

"You do have a way with words." Kaia slings her legs over the side of the mattress, then stands up.

"What does that mean?"

"Only a few people could make it sound like they're opening a door while confirming that it's still shut."

He shakes his head. "Kaia."

"It's okay," she says. "I knew what this was going in. You made that very clear." She gives him a tremulous smile, the best one she can muster. She doesn't want him to think that she's angry.

She's not, she's just…disappointed for reasons that don't quite make sense, considering they only just met.

"I'm going to come with you," he says, tossing the covers aside.

"What? No. You're not coming with me."

"Like hell I'm not," he argues. "It's still dark outside. I need to make sure you get home safely."

"Do you make sure your other one-night-stands get home safely?"

From the way his gaze casts downward toward the floor, Kaia knows that's a resounding 'no.'

"Then I don't want you to do that for me, okay?"

"If you don't want me to come with you, then my driver is going to drop you off at your apartment. I won't take no for an answer."

Kaia ignores him as she walks over to where her dress is in a pool on the floor. She slides it on, isn't really all that surprised when she feels the warmth of his body behind her, his fingers pulling the zipper closed.

"Kaia." His voice is too close for her liking. "Take the car."

"How do you have a car at your disposal at the hotel you take your..." 'Booty calls' is right at the tip of her tongue, but she doesn't say it. She doesn't want to be mean to him, especially when she's the one who's having second thoughts about the whole arrangement that he laid out very clearly.

The arrangement that she agreed to.

God. It was just sex. Why does she want to *stay*?

Just so he won't press her any further, she agrees. "Okay, I'll take the car."

"I'll call down to the front desk. Let me walk you."

She shakes her head. "No. Please don't. Let's just..."

Kaia wraps her arms around him, and kisses him for all

that she's worth. He responds eagerly, wrapping his body around hers, practically melting into her.

If this is all she can have of him, she's leaving with a souvenir.

"Kaia," he whispers.

She's certain Jason didn't mean for her to hear that.

She quickly grabs her shoes and her clutch, and walks out the door before she winds up doing something ridiculous, like trying to stay.

She came here looking for a good time, and she got exactly that. But never in a million years would she have ever guessed she'd leave here feeling so lonely.

Chapter 8

Jason sits in the far corner of a hip, crowded restaurant in San Francisco, even though his mind is 3,000 miles away, back in New York.

He can't stop thinking about Kaia, about how she looked before she left yesterday morning. About how he never wanted to break his own rule so badly, and how surprised he is that he regrets that he didn't.

He's driven to distraction by the thought of her, and he really, really needs to get over that. He has to find a way to get her out of his mind.

Across from him sits Elise Whittington, a woman who has known him his entire life. She was his mother's best friend and confidante, as well as Jason's Economics professor at Stanford. In the years since his mother has passed, Elise has been something like a maternal figure in Jason's life. She hasn't taken his mother's place, exactly, but she tries to be there for him in whatever way she can be.

Tonight, that includes a long-overdue reunion over dinner.

"Glad you finally made it in," she says, before taking a sip of her wine. "I was beginning to think that you telling me that your meeting was running over was code for nerves."

"Have I ever lied to you?"

Elise raises a brow. During his late teen years, when she and her husband were his guardians, he lied to her quite a bit.

"Just difficulty closing a deal," he replies nonchalantly. "No need to look into it any further than that."

Elise purses her lips together, a sign that Jason is all too familiar with from his childhood. He decides to derail the conversation and take control of it while he can.

"Thank you for inviting me here." He reaches for his drink. "I've never given a guest lecture before. I'm looking forward to it."

"Oh, please." Elise waves him off. "Getting the CEO of one of the largest investment firms in the world was huge for me, Jason. Especially one who's an alumnus? The lecture hall is going to be standing-room only."

Jason grins. "I hope I live up to everyone's expectations."

"I wouldn't have asked you to come all the way out here if I didn't think you could. Are you nervous at all?"

"Absolutely not," Jason replies, shaking his head. He thrives on the energy of a large crowd, loves the thrill of catching peoples attention and holding on tight.

Jason has the kind of swagger and self-assuredness that draws people in, that makes them want to listen to what he has to say. He's gotten pretty far in life using that skill, and has charmed money out of investors that way more times than he can count.

"Are you staying long?" Elise asks with her hope-filled voice.

Jason smiles softly at her, because he's about to give her an answer he knows she doesn't want to hear.

"No."

"So, this is a dine-n-dash, huh?" Elise aims for teasing, but sounds too hurt to pull it off.

Jason shakes his head. "Not really. I'm paying for dinner, giving the lecture in the morning, and *then* I'm dashing."

"You know what I mean," Elise says disapprovingly. "You're not even home for forty-eight hours."

What Jason can't bear to tell her is that this isn't his home anymore, that if tragedy hadn't made him want to leave and find a new life in New York, then he probably would've ended up there eventually anyway.

"I can't stay. There's a board meeting tomorrow, and I have some business I need to attend to before that. The sooner I catch my flight, the sooner I can get it taken care of."

"I've taught you well," Elise replies, sounding every bit the proud professor she is.

She takes a long, drawn-out sip of her red, watching Jason from over the rim of her glass. He knows from experience that this means an inquisition of sorts is in his very near future. He straightens his back, preparing himself for the onslaught.

"So, since it seems like this is the only time I'm going to have to spend with you this visit, fill me in on your life."

Jason relaxes a little. He was expecting something worse than a general request for information.

"There's not much to fill in. Work is going well. I've got a few new ventures I'm looking for investors for; I don't have anything shored up yet. My client base is growing, and thanks to you and your fellow educators doing a fine job with the graduate set, I'm able to hire a lot of talent right out of the gate."

"That's great," Elise replies with a genuine smile. "But that's not what I'm asking you. Business I can read in the newspaper, Jason. I'm asking about *your life*."

Jason knows exactly where this conversation is going, but he doesn't have an answer that she wants to hear.

"Why don't you ask me what you want to ask me, then."

"You're twenty-seven, Jason. I see your name pop up on gossip sites now and again, and you're always pictured with a different woman. I know that after what happened-"

"Elise," Jason warns, his whole body tensing.

She steels her shoulders and continues anyway.

"I know that after what happened that you're scared to form attachments to people, but you can't spend your life hopping from bed to bed-"

"Stop," he replies firmly. Not just because he absolutely

does not want to hear her opinion on his sex life, but because she's wrong about him and he can't stand to listen to another word of it. "I'm living my life the way I want to live it; my past doesn't have anything to do with that."

"Oh, sweetie," she says sympathetically. "How could it not?"

Jason hates the soft look in her eyes, the glassy reflection of the tears just waiting to be shed. He would do anything to avoid that look, the same one that people give him when they learn about what happened to him, to his family. It suggests a weakness, and if there's one thing he knows, it's that he's *not* weak.

He'll be damned if he lets anyone think he is.

"I'm young, and rich, and I have my pick of women to date. There isn't anything wrong with taking advantage of that."

"There isn't," Elise agrees cautiously. "But when you use that as an excuse not to form personal attachments because you think it's dangerous-"

"It *is* dangerous," Jason replies loudly, clapping his hand against the table top so hard that the glasses clink together. Even if he wasn't so attuned to his surroundings, he still wouldn't miss the way the chatter dies down after his outburst.

Still, he can see the curious eyes of the people in the restaurant settling on him. He leans forward, careful to keep his voice down and his temper under control. Elise has *never* understood his fear.

"It is *dangerous*, Elise," Jason says lowly. "I don't even like being here with *you*. You think I can fall in love while I'm constantly looking over my shoulder?"

Elise's eyes soften, and she reaches out and takes his hand.

"I think you wouldn't look over your shoulder so often if you had somewhere else to focus your attention. You wouldn't be so worried if you had a hand to hold. Living a life like this, without human connection, that's not what your par-"

"I have human connections," he argues, cutting her off.

"Not ones that stick. Not ones that matter."

Jason takes a deep breath, willing himself to calm down. "Can we not talk about this right now?"

"I love you, Jace. I just don't want you to be lonely. I don't want you to live your life thinking you're happy, then look back and wonder, 'what if?'"

"I don't wonder that."

"You never do, until it's too late to do anything about it. When you meet someone, and you want to stick around... stick around, okay? Don't live your life in self-imposed exile."

"Elise," he warns.

She opens her mouth like she's going to argue, but instead she sits back in her chair and nods.

Jason grips his whisky, and desperately tries not to think of Kaia, of the way her wavy hair felt against his bare skin. Of the way her lips tasted when she kissed him goodbye. Of the ache he feels when he remembers it.

No, he can't get lost in thoughts of a gorgeous blonde who made him laugh for the first time in what felt like years. A woman who made him feel a lightness in his chest that he thought was lost forever.

In the back of a town car that's stuck in midtown traffic on the way to his office from the airport, Jason thinks about his conversation with Elise.

He doesn't like to admit it, but maybe she was right. Before he met Kaia, he never felt lonely, never felt unfulfilled by a one-night stand. He reveled in the pleasure that was offered him knowing that he could find more when he wanted it. He's surprised by the fact that he wants *her*.

Again.

Maybe it will turn out to be nothing. Maybe they'll have dinner, and figure out that they aren't compatible. Maybe all that's in the cards for them is one more night of amazing sex, and a fond farewell.

Elise mentioned living without regrets, which is honestly something Jason never considered when it came to his personal life. He hasn't ever looked back and felt regret about a dalliance not becoming something more.

Over the past few days, he's been thinking about Kaia, going over their night together in meticulous detail. And when the car pulls up to the curb outside of his building, he looks at the spot where they ran into each other, where he effectively busted her computer all over the sidewalk, and actually feels a pang of longing for her.

Maybe it's the beginning of regret. Maybe it's a niggling of curiosity of what could be. He wants to find out.

The cold reality of why Elise was worried about Jason's personal life in the first place washes over him. If he lets himself care about someone, that person can be used against him. He feels the sting of pain long past, the reminder that history can repeat itself. Somewhere in the back of his mind, he can hear his mother's screams, his father begging, the sharp bite of the point of a gun pressed against his temple.

Jason has overcome considerable odds. If he puts his mind to something, he can achieve it. It's selfish, maybe, but he thinks he can keep Kaia safe. It'll be some work, but maybe finding out what could happen between them is worth it.

It surprises him when he realizes that he's not afraid of that.

Jason walks through the empty lobby of his office building, waving a quick hello to one of the weekend security guards before he makes his way into the executive elevator.

Sitting down at his desk, he catches sight of the Post-It Kaia wrote her address on the other day. He'd given the address to a courier to deliver her laptop right before he left for San Francisco, but held onto the paper for a reason he wasn't quite sure of at the time.

Now he knows: it was so he could find her again. He probably always knew deep down inside that he'd try.

He was going to try to get some work done this evening, but he can't wait another second longer.

Jason calls his driver, who meets him at the curb, his nerves on edge as they weave through traffic on the way to Kaia's place, which is a quaint little walkup off of a quiet street.

He tells his driver to wait for him at the end of the block: he'll text when and if he's ready to leave. Jason isn't sure what Kaia's reception is going to be like. Will she be glad to see him? What if she isn't home?

He should've asked for her number, but he had a rule about that.

Jason's going to break a lot of his rules tonight.

He catches the door to the lobby as one of the building's occupants walks out, grateful he doesn't have to buzz Kaia's apartment to be let in.

He makes his way up to the fifth floor in the cramped elevator, then steps out into the dimly-lit hallway.

Jason locates her door.

He knocks.

Chapter 9

"Now that you have that nice new computer, I figured you'd be doing some actual work on it instead of just staring at the wall."

Kaia realizes that Janine is talking to her a little too late, and looks up to see her roommate leaning against her doorway, looking at her patiently.

"What'd you say?"

Janine arches her brow. "Do you want to finally tell me what happened? You were so jazzed about your date, you spent the whole night out, and ever since you've come back you've been kind of a zombie."

"I'm not a zombie," Kaia replies defensively.

With a tilt of her head, Janine says, "You told me after lunch that you were coming in here to do some work, and the few times I've walked past, you've just been staring at the wall looking like, well…like that."

"Like what?"

Janine frowns a little, then looks off into the distance with a blank stare.

Kaia considers arguing that there's no way she's ever looked like that, but when she stops to think about it…she probably does look exactly that way.

Ever since Kaia left Jason's hotel room, her thoughts drift to him often. She knows that's ridiculous, considering he was up front with her about what he was and was not looking for, and he followed through with that. She has no right to be disappointed that he didn't want more, and yet, here she is, disappointed that he didn't want more.

Using the laptop that Jason gave her isn't exactly helping things. Every time she opens the lid, she remembers meeting him, remembers what happened after he gave it to her. It's so bad that she's considered selling it and using the money for a new one. But she'd probably think of the fact that she did that every time she tried typing on the new one, so she'd just wind up in an infinite loop of memories of a man she can't have.

The other morning when she came home from Jason's hotel room, she remembered giving him her address, and held out a little hope that he'd be the one who delivered the laptop to her. Imagine her disappointment after she heard a knock on the front door, only to open it and find a courier holding the package out to her with a friendly smile on his face.

"Just FYI, you're doing it again."

"Okay," Kaia relents. "I see what you mean. Sorry."

Janine gives her a soft smile as he walks over to the edge of Kaia's bed, then slowly sits down.

"Wanna tell me what happened?"

"I already did," Kaia says softly.

"You said that he didn't want to pursue anything. I think there's more to it than that."

"There isn't, trust me."

Janine scoots closer to Kaia on the bed. "I don't believe you."

Kaia sighs. "He told me he doesn't do relationships right up front."

"You mean, you got all dressed up to go on a date, and were so excited for it when you knew there wasn't even the possibility that the guy would commit?" Janine's brows are furrowed, because she knows Kaia well, and definitely knows that is so unlike her.

"No, I got all dressed up to go on a date, then showed up at the guy's place. He made me come so hard I couldn't see straight, and then he told me he wouldn't commit, but offered me one night together."

Janine looks shocked. "And you agreed?"

Kaia flushes, and toys with the edge of her comforter. "If you had been me, you would've agreed. I don't want to be too graphic, but his hands were so talented that I just had to find out what the rest of him could do."

"He sounds rude," Janine replies.

"How so?"

"Well," she says, tapping her chin. "Either rude or a complete genius."

"Janine," Kaia warns.

"He gives you a taste of the goods, then lets you know they're only available for a limited-time offer. Okay, I've decided. Not rude, definitely genius."

Kaia can't really argue with that assessment. "I agreed to it knowing nothing would ever come of us being together, but after..." she trails off, feeling wistful at the thought.

"After what?" Janine asks impatiently.

Kaia shrugs. "He told me he had an early flight, but that if he didn't he would've wanted to have breakfast with me."

"What?" Janine's face screws up in something that resembles shock mixed with confusion. "He led you on?"

"Not really."

"Yes, really. He tells you that you can't have more, but then says, 'Oh, but I would if I could!' Asshole."

Kaia can't help but laugh at that. "He laid out the rules. Besides, it's silly to get all emotional over a guy I knew for less than a day. I just thought..."

"It's not silly," Janine replies, reaching for Kaia's hand. "I think the knowing you can't have him makes you want him even more."

Kaia's pretty sure she has a point there. "Looking at this computer doesn't help."

"If you want, tomorrow morning we can take it to the park

and smash it into pieces. The weapons of destruction are on me."

"Tempting offer," Kaia says with a laugh. "But I do actually need something to do my work on."

"Pity. But it's an open-ended offer, in case you ever change your mind."

Kaia smiles. "I'll keep that in mind."

"Since you're clearly not going to get any work done tonight, why don't we order an obscene amount of Chinese food, drink the last of the wine in the fridge, and watch some movies with happy endings?"

Kaia gives Janine a teasing look.

"The happily ever after kind of happy endings, not the sexual kind."

Kaia laughs. "That sounds good."

"Why don't you put on your jammies, and I'll call the Szechuan place down the street?"

With a nod, Kaia hums out her agreement. "Okay."

There's a knock on the door, and Janine sighs.

"First I'll get the door, *then* I'll order the food."

Kaia shuts down her laptop, carefully closes the lid, and places it on her nightstand.

"Hey. Kaia." Janine is whispering in some weird, clipped, excited way.

"Yeah?"

"Someone's at the door for you." Her eyes are wide and excited.

"Who?"

Janine turns back toward the living room.

"Jason," she whispers.

Kaia's heart skips a beat.

Kaia stands awkwardly in her living room, which seems so small and cramped with a larger-than-life kind of guy like Jason in the middle of it. Jason's hands are in his pockets, and he looks completely casual, like this is something he does every day.

Meanwhile, Kaia's heart is about to beat out of her chest. Her fingers are twined together behind her back, and she mainly focuses her attention on the floor, occasionally looking up and giving Jason a shy smile.

She's afraid of making any other kind of move, afraid of what she might say with Janine in the other room.

"I'm gonna go out for some ice cream," Janine says, as she walks out of her bedroom, pulling on a hoodie. She's still wearing her pajamas, and Kaia's pretty sure she doesn't realize that. "Maybe a drink? But probably just ice cream. Or whatever I need to get that will keep me out long enough for you to do whatever it is that you need to do."

"We're not going to do anything," Kaia replies, desperate for her friend to shut up.

"Oh…kay." Janine is frantically searching for her purse.

"On the counter."

Janine's gaze shoots over there. "The counter, right."

She walks over and slings the bag across her shoulder as she makes her way toward the door.

Butterflies are flapping their wings against Kaia's stomach, and she's trembling a little. Part of her is desperate for Janine to leave, but the other part wants her to stay for some moral support.

"I'll see you later," Janine says to Kaia with a smile. She's a great roommate, giving Kaia some time alone with Jason, but Kaia can't help but think she's a little bit of a traitor. She'll forgive her tomorrow, probably. She grins at Jason. "It was nice to meet you."

Jason grins back. "You, too."

Kaia watches as Janine slips out the door. When she's out of Jason's line of sight, she gives Kaia a wide-eyed, excited look.

"Oh my god," she mouths silently, then holds up her cell phone. "Text me later."

Then the door shuts, and it's just the two of them.

"Sorry to just show up without calling," he explains smoothly. "But I don't have your number."

A little niggle of annoyance pulls at Kaia's stomach. "That's because you didn't ask for it," she says, trying to stay light. "Because you don't...what were the words? You don't *do relationships*?" She just barely manages not to make sarcastic air quotes.

Kaia tries desperately to rein herself in by reminding herself that she has no right to be annoyed or angry. He spelled out the terms of their night together very clearly before she agreed to them.

And, she also reminds herself. *It was just one night.* For the life of her, she can't figure out why it felt like so much more, like the two of them were standing on the edge of something great, but Jason just wasn't willing to jump.

Jason has the nerve to let out a little breath that sounds somewhere in the vicinity of a laugh. Then he reaches out and crooks his fingers below Kaia's chin, sliding the pad of his thumb along the curve of her lower lip.

"I did say that," he replies, his voice low.

"And then you used a business trip that might or might not have been real to tease a little, then take it back."

Jason nods. "I did do that, and I'm sorry."

The apology surprises Kaia. Not that she has any experience with it, but she didn't think that men in his position apologized all that much.

"Here to check up on your laptop, then?" she asks icily, cringing at the way her voice sounds. She's being a bitch to him, and she knows it.

She doesn't want to be a bitch, she's just...confused.

Jason's eyes soften. "That's *your* laptop. And no. I'm here for you."

She feels a pull deep in her belly. It's excitement, and a little bit of hesitation.

"What?" she says, not fully understanding.

Jason steps forward, into Kaia's personal space. He reaches

up, and traces his fingertips along her hairline, making a shiver run up and down her spine. She closes her eyes against his touch, remembering all the lovely things his fingers can do, what they felt like running across her body…

"I should've never let you leave that morning. I can't stop thinking about you."

Kaia revels in his touch, before opening her eyes and taking a step back. She can't let herself get too wrapped up in this man now that she knows how easily this whole thing can slip between her fingers.

The movement surprises Jason, and Kaia sees his expression fall before he's able to hide it.

Kaia squares her shoulders, wanting to be strong here. She feels like so much is riding on whatever happens next, and as much as she wants him, she knows she can't just give in.

"So what does that mean? You want a relationship with me?" She goes right for the jugular, for what she knows will make him uncomfortable, so she can read his true intentions.

It works; she can see his Adam's apple bob as he swallows. He recovers quickly.

"I was thinking more of a trial run."

"You mean more sex, with no commitment."

"No," he says shaking his head. "I mean dating, more sex, and possible commitment."

Kaia presses her lips together. All-in-all, this doesn't sound like a bad offer, as long as it's a sincere one.

"You mean it, you're not…you're not just trying to get me

back into bed."

Jason narrows his eyes, and looks at her intensely.

"I'm definitely trying to get you back in bed."

Kaia turns, not wanting to play any games, but Jason tangles his fingers with hers before she can get away.

"Don't walk away from me, Kaia."

She doesn't want to. But she doesn't want to be screwed around with, either.

"If that was *all* I wanted I would tell you. I'm a complicated man, Kaia, there are…there are a lot of things you don't know about me. Things I'm not sure I'll ever be willing to share. But I won't lie to you. Not ever."

"Okay…" Kaia says, still not sure where exactly he's going with this.

"If this was going to be a casual thing for me, I would tell you that up front."

Kaia nods, she understands this. She believes him, too, because he's already been up front with her about his intent to keep things casual.

He continues. "I'm telling you that I'm trying to make myself open to the possibility of more, but don't want to miss my opportunity."

Kaia takes a deep breath, and absorbs everything he's telling her. "So, what you're saying is that you're trying to get yourself used to the idea of dating someone, and you want me to be available to you, you just don't want me to date anyone else."

Jason stares at Kaia, his eyes dark and deep and full of possessiveness.

"Yes," he replies, his voice raspy. "That's exactly what I'm saying."

What he wants is for her to hang on to maybes, and Kaia isn't sure she wants to do that. But the sex was *so* good, and she's been living with this inexplicable nagging ache of 'what if' in her belly ever since she left his hotel room that night. It's not like she has any other prospects at the moment…

"Jason." Her tone is a little pleading, because it's a difficult situation for her. Then again, saying yes to maybes, means saying yes to more of some truly excellent, mind-blowing sex.

"I want you," Jason says firmly. "I don't want anyone else to have you." He cups her face, then lets his hand slide down the curve of her neck, across her collarbone, down the swell of her breast.

His thumb brushes across her nipple, and even through her shirt and her bra, it makes her shiver. All the resolve she's been holding together just…crumbles.

"Okay."

Jason leans forward, with a sly, seductive grin on his stupidly handsome face.

He kisses Kaia long, and slow, and deep, 'til she thinks her heart might beat out of her chest.

When Jason pulls away, he whispers, "I promise I'll make it worth your while."

Chapter 10

"What do you mean you're not coming?"

Chase Jennings, Jason's oldest friend, sits beside him at the bar, gripping a frosty bottle of beer between his fingers.

Jason takes a pull from his own bottle, then sets it down in front of him.

"I mean exactly what I said," Jason replies. "Something came up."

"It's not like you to cancel on me last minute, especially not for a party like this. Remember all the models that showed up last year? We can have our pick."

Jason takes a deep breath, then tilts his head forward, trying to loosen the knot that's forming between his shoulder blades.

"I can't," he says again, adamantly, while smiling at his

friend.

"You're missing out."

"Doubtful." The words came automatically, and if Jason had a second to think about what he was doing, he never would've let himself say them. But, it's too late.

"What is going on with you? If I didn't know better, I'd think you…"

Jason sees the look of surprise on Chase's face, even out of the corner of his eye.

"Holy shit," Chase says with a laugh.

"What?"

"You're seeing someone." Chase says it with a hint of accusation, like he's certain he's figured out something that Jason's been hiding.

And he has.

"I'm not." He and Kaia haven't seen each other since he left her apartment the night before last, but he's seeing her tonight, and the lie feels wrong coming out of his mouth.

"Bullshit. You are."

Jason doesn't want to lie again, so he says nothing.

"Never thought I'd see the day."

When Jason turns and looks at his friend, he's grinning like a moron.

"What day?"

"You in a relationship. Even though it's been fun being your wingman, I have to admit that it's good to see that you're admitting you might be wrong about your rule."

"I'm not admitting anything."

With a smile, Chase shakes his head, and brings his bottle up to his lips. "Elise finally get through to you?"

Jason isn't really sure how to talk about this. He's not big on expressing his feelings, and he definitely doesn't want word circulating that he's seeing someone. He trusts Chase, it's just that this is all so new, and he didn't make Kaia any promises about what would come next. It could be over by this time next week for all he knows.

And it would be safer if it's a secret. But the more he denies it, the deeper Chase will try to dig.

"I met someone," he says carefully. "But it's new, and none of your goddamn business. So keep it to yourself." He tries not to grin as he says the words, but Chase understands.

"Really? Wow."

"What?"

"Does she know about everything?"

"Chase," he warns. His friend is almost as bad as Elise.

"You're going to have to tell her, you know that, right? If she hasn't asked already because of the-"

"I'll tell her when I'm ready to tell her. If she's still around by that point."

His oldest friend looks him in the eye, and Jason knows he's not going to like what comes next.

"It doesn't make you damaged goods, you know. Not everyone is Skylar, man. Not every woman is going to disappear when they find out."

Jason isn't so sure that he's right, and he's not willing to risk it yet. "I said it's none of your business. When I'm ready to tell her, I'll tell her."

"Hey," Chase says, holding his hands up in mock surrender. "Your secret's safe with me. But I'm happy for you, man." Chase reaches over and claps Jason on the back. "I'm gonna have to find another partner in crime, though."

"Somehow I think you'll live."

"I might," Chase says with a laugh. "Have fun tonight."

Jason grins. "I plan on it."

"Wow," Kaia says, looking up at the ceiling in his loft. "This place is…wow." She walks over to the windows, and takes a look at the view. The light from the skyscrapers around them are bright around her silhouette.

Jason was nervous about bringing her up here. He's never had a woman in his apartment before. Since he's so accustomed to one-night stands, he usually goes to the woman's place, or makes use of the room the Drake has on hold for him.

His home was his sanctuary.

And now Kaia is standing right in the middle of it.

It feels comfortable in a way that he never thought possible, and is a little weirded out by, considering they've only just met.

Jason is holding a glass of wine for each of them, the stems anchored between his fingers. But as Kaia stands there and watches the city below them, he stands there and watches her.

She's in a figure-hugging black dress, her hair tumbling over her shoulders, looking just as breathtakingly gorgeous as he remembered. He wants her *so* much, wants to taste her skin under his tongue, to feel the wet warmth of her as he sheathes himself inside of her body.

He surprises himself by wanting to sit down and actually talk to her, too.

Jason walks up behind her, then leans forward and presses a soft kiss against her shoulder. She hums, and he can feel her shiver.

"Is red okay?" he asks as he hands her a glass.

"It's perfect." She turns and gives him a soft smile before she takes a sip, then lets out a soft hum after she swallows. "Thank you."

"You look beautiful."

God help him; she blushes as she gives him a soft smile.

"Thank you."

He leans in and gives her a kiss because he can't help himself, his free hand sliding up into her soft hair. Their tongues tangle, and he has to reel himself in before he gets lost in her.

When he pulls away, he rests his forehead against Kaia's as he catches his breath.

"Wow," Kaia breathes.

"You seem to be saying that a lot tonight."

She leans back, her eyebrows furrowed. "When did I say it before?"

"Shortly after you walked in," Jason replies with a grin.

"Oh, yeah. Well, this place is *wow*. It's not at all what I expected."

Jason takes her hand and leads her over to sit beside him on the couch. "What were you expecting?"

"Armored guards or something?" she says, laughing a little with embarrassment. "I mean, I don't know how rich you are, but you own a building in Manhattan, and obviously have money, and I thought…oh God, I'm going to shut up."

Jason finds himself charmed by her candor. "Please, keep talking."

She really is blushing now, and Jason thinks it's lovely.

"I don't want you to kick me out."

He reaches up, and cups her cheek. "I would never. You're actually the first woman I've had up here."

Kaia blanches. "Ever?"

"Yes."

"No way."

Jason takes a sip of his wine, then sets it on the table next to him. "I told you I wouldn't lie to you, Kaia."

"Wow," she says again.

"So get back to what you were saying before. What were you expecting when you walked in here?"

"Honestly?" she asks, like she's giving him one last chance to change his mind.

He nods. "Honestly."

"I was expecting Fort Knox-level security. Like retinal

scans and guards, and lots and lots of gold."

Jason lets out a surprised laugh. "The best security is the kind you never see." And it's true; this is probably the safest place she'll ever be, and that's the reason why he asked her here this evening instead of inviting her out to dinner.

"And all the gold?" she teases.

"Never really cared for it."

Kaia nods with a smile as she brings her glass up to her lips again.

"So, tell me about yourself," Jason says.

Kaia raises her brow. "Really? We're doing this?"

"Getting to know each other? I thought that was what you wanted?"

"It is," she says quickly. "I just…I didn't think that was what we were going to do here."

"You thought I just wanted to to fuck you."

Her cheeks heat at the words he chooses, but her eyes remain steadily on his. "Yes."

"I told you that I wouldn't promise anything, but that I'd like to try."

"I know, it's just…a little surreal to be sitting here with you actually doing this."

Jason can't help but smile. He knows what she's feeling.

"Tell me about yourself, Kaia." Jason isn't going to let her avoid this.

"Didn't you run a background check on me before you invited me over?"

Jason lets out an incredulous laugh. "No, I didn't."

"Really?"

"Really. Did you run a background check on me?"

Kaia presses her lips together guiltily.

"You did?"

"If you consider looking you up on the internet a background check. I just wanted to make sure you weren't a criminal."

"What did you find?" he asks, curious.

"That you're twenty seven, you own a Fortune 500 investment firm. You graduated from Stanford with honors, and that you came in second place at some pro-am golf thing upstate."

Jason chuckles. "That's quite the list."

"It is. Sadly there isn't much about you in your younger years. I was looking for an embarrassing pic or two, but nothing. You must've been quite unremarkable."

He freezes on instinct, and hopes like hell that he covers it before Kaia notices. There is a reason why she can't find anything on him when he was younger; he's done his very best to erase the younger version of him from existence.

"Very unremarkable," he says, trying to sound light, but probably failing spectacularly.

She seems amused by him, and he gets the sense that she didn't notice him tense earlier.

"Still don't want to admit to looking me up?"

Jason shakes his head. "Nope. I only want to know what

you want to tell me."

From the small smile on her face, Jason knows that was the correct answer. It also helps that it's the truth.

"Okay."

"So," he says, trying again. "Tell me."

"I grew up in Des Moines; my older sister still lives there with my parents. I'm twenty two, and I graduated from Syracuse this past spring." She pauses at the end, her gaze moving up to the ceiling, like she's trying to figure out what else to say. "I'm not very good at talking about myself."

Jason finds that endearing, because the women he usually spends time with (regardless of how limited it is) have no trouble talking about themselves at all. In fact, they have trouble *stopping*.

These are things he could find out about her on the internet if he felt compelled to look. He wants *more*.

"Tell me something else," Jason says, moving closer to her, so their knees are touching.

"Like what?" She looks up at him, her eyelashes fanning across her lids. The wine is giving her cheeks color, and he wants to kiss her and never stop.

"Not sure; what do you want me to know?"

She smiles, then thinks on it. "Like facts?"

Jason smiles back at her. "Yes, all the facts."

"I hate peanut butter, but I love peanut butter cookies."

Jason laughs. This is exactly what he's looking for. Things that make Kaia *Kaia*. "Okay."

"I have this sweater that I love, and it's so comfortable that sometimes I wear it for three days straight." She looks at him out of the corner of her eye, like she's expecting him to be revolted.

"I'd like to see this sweater."

"When I was a kid, my dad convinced me that the closer you lived to the beach, the more likely it was that fish would come out of your faucet."

Jason actually cracks up at that, and he can't wait anymore. He leans in and kisses her.

Chapter 11

Kaia is lying naked on Jason's incredibly huge, incredibly comfortable bed, propped up on her elbows.

City lights stream into the windows, casting shadows on all the places it can't touch. Jason is standing before her, knees touching the edge of the bed, his glorious body on full display.

"Spread your legs for me."

His voice is low, and rough, and it sent a thrill shooting through Kaia's body.

"Do it," he says firmly. "Now. Don't make me wait."

She does as he asks immediately, watches the desire flood his eyes as he looks at her, wet and ready for him.

"You're beautiful," he says, with such conviction that she believes him. "I've been thinking about you ever since that night. The way you tasted, how your skin felt beneath my hands."

He slides his palms up the insides of Kaia's thighs, making goosebumps break out all over her skin. The pad of his thumb brushes across her clit, and she sucks in a big breath of air between her teeth.

Jason drops to his knees before her, then wraps his arms around her hips and pulls her down, so her ass is nearly hanging off the edge of the bed.

Kaia reaches forward and rakes her nails across Jason's scalp, and he hums as he presses short, hot kisses across her bikini line.

"I've been thinking about you, too," she says, running her fingers through his hair since he seems to like that so much.

"Yeah?"

"Oh yeah. You were..." She's about to tell him that he's the best sex she's ever had, but she doesn't want to inflate his ego.

"I was what?" he asks. His thumb brushes against her clit again, and Kaia rocks her hips forward. "Tell me, or I'll stop."

Oh, he's mean. There's a daring glint in his eyes that lets her know that he's totally serious, too.

"That night," she begins, still seeking out some friction. "No one's ever made me..." Kaia doesn't know why she's feeling so shy right now. She's in the most vulnerable position she can possibly be in, with Jason's head between her thighs.

"No one ever made you come before I did?" He seems taken aback, almost offended on her behalf.

"No," Kaia says, smiling. "I've had orgasms before, just not like the ones I had that night. You…you were the best. So far."

A dark look of desire slides across Jason's face as he slides two fingertips along Kaia's wet slit, then pushes them inside.

She lets out a long, soft sigh as he lowers his mouth to her, sucking and licking on her clit in perfect timing with his fingers. The stubble above Jason's upper lip is providing the *best* friction, and Kaia has to basically stop herself from grinding against his face. Her hips stutter as she fights off her instinct to seek more pleasure from this man.

And then, it stops. Kaia actually whimpers at the loss of his mouth.

"Kaia," he says, as he reaches up and cups her breast, tweaking her nipple between his fingers. "Why are you holding back?"

"I'm not," she lies.

Jason narrows his eyes at her. "Don't be shy with me. I can't make you feel as good as I want to if you're stopping yourself from letting it happen."

"Your stubble feels good," Kaia admits.

Jason slowly kneads her breast. "Yeah?"

Kaia nods.

"Why is that a problem?"

"I don't want to grind on your face."

Jason lets out a husky laugh, and the warm breath fanning against the inside of her thigh makes Kaia shiver.

"If grinding on my face is going to make you come, then grind on my face."

"I..."

Jason stands, and leans over Kaia, pressing his hands on the mattress beside her shoulders for leverage.

He kisses her, long and slow and deep. She gets lost in it, can taste herself on his tongue. Jason presses his chest against hers, and the sparse hair on his chest stimulates her nipples, making her writhe beneath him.

"Let go," he whispers against her lips. "Let me make you feel good."

His hips rock against hers, his hard cock heavy and warm on her thigh. He kisses his way down her chest, licking her nipple, swirling his tongue around her belly button.

By the time Jason is settled back between her thighs, she's lighter than air, her brain is completely shut off, and she's only focusing on the sensations of what he's doing to her body.

Kaia crushes a handful of sheets between her fingers as Jason works her clit, and she rocks her hips with abandon, climbing higher and higher and higher.

She comes with a shout, her back arching up off of the bed, and Jason twines his fingers through hers as she comes down to give her something to hold onto.

"I grew up in California," Jason says, breaking the silence between them.

Kaia is spooned against his body, their legs tangled together, Jason's arms wrapped around her in a safe cocoon.

She slides her hands up and down his forearm, where it's slung across her chest.

She's not sure what to say to that revelation. She wants to know more, but doesn't want to pry. He's made it quite clear that this is all new to him, and the very last thing Kaia wants to do is push him too far.

"That sounds lovely," she replies. Seems benign enough.

Jason lets out a low, rumbly laugh. Kaia can feel the vibration of it against her back.

"Why are you laughing?" She teasingly swats at his arm.

"All I mentioned was the state. How do you know I didn't grow up in a real slum?"

"You didn't grow up in a slum," Kaia replies confidently. "And if you'd spent most of your life in a landlocked state, California would sound great to you, too."

"Fair enough," Jason replies, nuzzling his nose into her hair.

"What made you leave?"

Jason stills, and it takes Kaia a split second to realize that she might have asked the wrong question.

"You don't have to answer that, I-"

"It's fine," he replies quietly. "Don't tiptoe around me. You can ask me anything you like, but I might not always answer."

Kaia nods. "Okay."

"I left because I wanted to start a new life, to get away from the weight of expectations. Some good, some bad. The city always felt like home to me."

She wants to ask him if his family is still there. She wonders if that's who he went to visit when he went to San Francisco the other day. These, however, are questions that aren't any of her business yet, and regardless, she's certain that they fall under the category of those he won't answer.

She doesn't file them away for good, she just files them away for another day.

"The city always felt like home to me, too," Kaia replies, trying to steer the conversation to a more comfortable place for Jason. "That's why I moved here with my roommate Janine after college. My parents did *not* approve."

"What did they want you to do?" he asks, his lips skimming across Kaia's shoulder.

"They wanted me to come back to Iowa. They were upset that I left in the first place, but Syracuse gave me a full ride. I knew that if I didn't get out then, I never would."

"I know what that feels like," Jason replies.

At least Jason would've had the means to get out of whatever situation he found himself stuck in, but Kaia doesn't voice the thought.

"I wanted to see the world, and figured that the city was the best starting point."

Kaia feels Jason's smile against her skin. "It is. I can attest to that."

"I bet you've seen a lot of it."

"I have." Jason adjusts his hold on her, so that his rough palm is sliding across her breasts. Kaia arches back into him, can feel his erection against her ass. He presses short, soft kisses across her shoulder. "I can show you places you've never even dreamed of, Kaia."

"Yeah?"

"Mmm…" he hums as his hand snakes across the curve of her hip, to the inside of her thigh. He lifts her leg, giving him full access to her. He slides his fingertips across her slit, already wet and ready for him. "I can and I will."

Kaia hands him a condom, and waits patiently for him to roll it on.

He rubs the tip of his cock against her clit, and Kaia impatiently rocks against him, desperate for friction.

"Please don't tease me," she says, marveling at how fast they went from sharing tiny pieces of their lives to her desire for him rapidly spiraling out of control.

"What do you want me to do?" he asks, with a growl in her ear.

"Fuck me. I want you to fuck me."

Jason plunges inside of her, and Kaia lets out a cry as his hips pound against her. He presses his hand against her belly, making each thrust feel deeper than it has before. Kaia closes her eyes as Jason rubs her clit, and sucks on the spot just below her ear that drives her crazy.

He promised to show her places she's never dreamed of.

Tonight, she'll settle for seeing stars.

Chapter 12

Jason walks out of his closet, fastening his cufflinks as morning sun begins to stream through his bedroom window. Kaia is sleeping soundly in his bed. Her hair is a gorgeous mess spread across his pillows, and the sheet is wrapped around her chest, dipping low and exposing most of her left breast.

He has to get to the office, but what he'd really like is to crawl back into bed with her, wrap his body around hers and memorize the way his name sounds when she shouts it as she comes.

The thought chills him. He's always been perfectly able to distance himself from women, because he's never allowed himself to get attached. He's only known Kaia for less than a week, and he knows he's in danger.

He's felt this overwhelming connection with her ever since

they first met, and he can't deny wanting to be around her as much as he can. For the first time in his adult life, he doesn't feel the overwhelming desire to distance himself from her, to keep his options open. He doesn't want to run her out of his bed to free up the rest of his day; instead he finds himself wishing he could linger.

He told her he wasn't going to make any promises, and he still isn't, but he's falling for her…fast.

He can tell she's curious about his life, but doesn't want to push him. She's giving him room to ease into things. Last night, after he made her come a third time, she tried to get up and leave, thinking he wouldn't want her spending the night.

He gently pulled her back into bed, and asked her to stay. It was definitely unlike him, but if he was going to put her in danger, he was damn sure going to keep her safe. He'd rather she be here than at her apartment.

If only she knew how on-the-nose her comment about security was last night. Jason told her the truth: the best security is the kind you can't see, and exactly the kind he employs.

Truthfully, he didn't just want her to stay so he could keep an eye on her; he wanted her to stay because he liked the feeling of waking up with her in his arms, and wanted to experience it again.

He also knows that if she had a clear idea of what she was getting into with him, she might not be so willing to stay after all. And if she knew about his past, she might run screaming.

He shakes his head, not wanting to overthink things, not wanting to make a problem where one doesn't exist yet.

Regardless of what happens in the future, he has to wake her up now, or he'll be late to his first meeting of the day.

Jason walks over to the side of the bed, and sits down on the edge, watching Kaia breathe steadily in and out, her face so beautifully peaceful. He finds himself wishing he knew whether she likes waking up to the smell of coffee or tea, whether she's a morning person, or whether he can expect her to be grumpy with him.

He figures the best way to rouse her is to do it slowly, so he gently slides his fingertips down the curve of her jaw.

"Kaia," he whispers, cupping her cheek.

She lets out a soft hum, then cuddles against the warmth of his hand. Just that small action of trust makes Jason smile.

"You have to wake up." His voice is a little louder this time, and he can tell by the way Kaia's eyebrows scrunch together that she's waking. He swipes his thumb across her cheekbone, and she goes from sleepy to wide-awake in an instant.

"Oh my god," she says frantically. "I didn't mean to stay, I-"

"Relax," Jason replies soothingly. "I asked you to stay, remember?"

Kaia's shoulders loosen, and she looks at him with sleepy, tired eyes. Jason thinks it's probably one of the most adorable things he's ever seen.

"Yeah. I remember now."

Jason smiles at her, leans in and gives her a soft, quick kiss.

"I have to go soon. I have a meeting."

Kaia's expression falls just a little, doubt creeping in around the edges, and he feels the need to reassure her. She probably thinks that meetings are his go-to excuse, since he used one to explain why he couldn't take her to breakfast the other day.

"Hey," he says. "This is part of whatever it is that we're doing here. I have meetings almost every day. I'm not...I'm not trying to get out of anything or make excuses, okay?"

The corner of Kaia's mouth tips up into a small smile. "Okay."

He leans in to kiss her again, but Kaia turns away from him.

"What?"

"Pretty sure there's some morning breath going on here."

"I don't care," Jason replies, as he cups Kaia's cheek and turns her head so he has better access to her lips.

"Good morning," Kaia says with a smile, as Jason pulls away.

"Great morning."

"I'm just gonna..." She motions to her current state of undress, and Jason lets out a little groan. He's never wanted to call in sick so badly. But his company needs him, and if he's going to make this work, he can't let himself get distracted like this. It takes every bit of willpower he has in him to stand up, but he does it.

"Would you like some coffee? Or tea?"

Kaia gives him a grateful look. "Coffee would be great. A

little cream, a little sugar?"

Jason nods and stands, then walks out of the room before every ounce of resolve he has completely disappears.

Jason barely finishes making Kaia's coffee before she's walking out of his bedroom looking less put together than she had when she came over last night, but no less gorgeous. Her hair is piled into a messy bun on the top of her head, and her makeup is smudged a little around her eyes.

She walks into the kitchen, standing next to Jason at the counter where he's tightening the lid on her coffee.

"A travel mug and everything?" she asks, teasing.

"I wanted to make sure it stays hot."

Kaia breathes in and lets out a low hum. "Mmmm, I do have a long train ride home."

"No you don't," he replies. "My driver is going to drop you off."

"Jason, no."

"Yes, I insist."

Kaia shakes her head. "I can't take advantage. That's not… it isn't important to me that you do that."

"It's important to *me*," he explains. He can't tell her why - not yet, maybe not ever, depending - but he needs her to agree. "It's part and parcel of whatever this is, whatever it becomes."

"Is this something to do with you not wanting people to know you're seeing someone who isn't…are you trying to keep up appearances?"

That surprises Jason, and he isn't able to hide it. "What? No. It's just something that I need you to do, okay?" He's fighting the urge to insist that she have her own driver full time. Maybe it'll come to that, depending on how serious this thing between them becomes, but for now he's going to take this one step at a time. "Please."

With no small amount of reluctance, she finally agrees. "Okay."

Jason smiles, and wraps her in his arms. "Thank you."

Kaia hugs him, then leans back and runs the palm of her hand over his stubble. He closes his eyes at the sensation, at the intimacy of it.

"You're welcome," she replies, then stretches up on her tiptoes and presses her lips against his.

Her mouth is minty and warm, and Jason feels her melting against his body as he wraps her up tight in the safety of his embrace.

"Mmmm," he hums when they part.

"I used a little bit of your toothpaste." Her eyes widen, and she continues with, "*not* your tooth brush. Just the toothpaste."

Jason grins at her, feeling the lightness in his chest spread out to his fingertips.

"I want to see you tonight," he says, before giving her another kiss. "May I?"

"You may." Her lips brush against his as she speaks.

"I'll pick you up at seven; we'll have dinner at my place."

"Okay."

"Bring your toothbrush," Jason says with a happy lilt in his voice. "I'll supply the toothpaste."

"Oooh," Kaia says with a delighted laugh. "Another sleepover."

Jason's hand slides down her side, the pad of his thumb teasing the swell of Kaia's breast. He drags his stubble across her cheek, and leans in close to her ear. "We won't be doing much sleeping."

Kaia plays with the hair at the nape of Jason's neck, and gives him a sexy smile. "Looking forward to it."

"Me too. Let me walk you down."

In the elevator, Jason slides his hand up and down Kaia's back, relishing in the comfort of her nearness, getting every ounce of togetherness he can before they part for the day. It scares him how easy it is to fall into this, to want more and to take it, and to really make a go of things between them.

He's fought it for so long, but finding the right person makes letting go so easy. He thinks he's found that in Kaia.

He just hopes that neither one of them winds up regretting it.

The elevator lets them out in the building's basement, and Jason leads Kaia into the garage, where a driver is standing with the back door open, ready to usher her in.

Jason gives Kaia a quick peck as he helps her in, then makes sure she's settled inside. It isn't until the car disappears up the ramp that leads out to the street that Jason walks over to a large man in a fancy suit with stiff posture, standing to the right of the door.

"You've got eyes on her?" Jason asks.

The man - Paul, head of his security team - gives Jason a solemn nod.

"Two of my best guys - they're in a car behind her. The driver knows not to lose them."

"I don't want her stalked, I just need her safe. Don't violate her privacy, just-"

"We've got it handled, Sir," Paul replies with confidence.

Jason knows this. He had a long discussion with Paul about what exactly he was expecting from him and his team when he asked for a small detail for Kaia.

He just...he has to make sure. He'll never forgive himself if something happens to her. He can take someone coming after him, but not her. He won't allow it.

If allowing himself a relationship with Kaia resulted in her getting hurt in any way...

Jason shakes his head, doesn't let himself entertain thoughts like that.

Kaia has the best security in the world looking out for her, and for now that has to be enough.

Chapter

13

It doesn't take very long for Kaia and Jason to get into a routine. They see each other just about every night, have mind-blowing sex, and then lie in each other's arms, talking about everything and nothing at all until sleep finally takes them.

The sex is great, it's wonderful, but the after—when she's wrapped up in the safety of Jason's arms—that's quickly becoming her favorite part. It's when she learns the most about him, when he's most willing to open up to her.

She learns little things about him: that he's always hated Brussels sprouts, his favorite color is blue, he doesn't like sitting next to the window on an airplane. He's very slowly starting to open up to her about the big things, too, like the fact that his beloved grandmother died in a car accident when he was twelve, and that he set up a charity so he could anonymously donate money to employees who had sick children, and had difficulty paying their medical bills.

Every night she spends in his arms, she gets to know a little bit more about him.

Every night, she falls for him a little bit more. It's happening fast, but Kaia's so wrapped up in him and the euphoria she feels just being around him that she doesn't stop to think about all that; she just wants *more*.

Tonight, they're lying together in Jason's bed, naked and sated. Jason is on his back, and Kaia's all tucked up against his side, her head resting on his shoulder.

"I don't want you seeing anyone else," he says, out of the blue.

A short little thrill lights its way out to her fingertips and toes. "Yeah?"

The pillowcase ruffles as Jason nods. "Yeah."

"And who are you seeing in this scenario?" she asks, aiming for teasing, but not quite sure she gets there.

"Just you. I only want to see you."

The thrill intensifies, and Kaia can't hide her smile. She doesn't want to.

"Yeah? We're making this official?" She's teasing again, but there's some truth in this question. Till now, their dates have consisted of dinner that's been ordered in, and dark booths in the backs of exclusive restaurants where they sneaked in through the back door.

If they're going to have a relationship, Kaia wants it to be something that's out in the open, something that she can share.

Jason is quiet, and Kaia immediately knows she's said something wrong.

"I was just teasing, I-"

"I know what this looks like," he replies quietly, body tense.

"You're a guy who used to show up in the tabloids with a different woman every night. To me, it looks like you're trying to do things differently now."

"I am," he admits.

"I'm not going to pressure you into anything, but…I won't hide. If that's what you want me to do, if you're looking for a secret, then-"

"I'm not, that's not it. I just need a little more time before we…"

"Go public?"

Jason lets out a short huff of a laugh. "Yeah."

"Okay, then." She's absentmindedly tracing one of the scars over Jason's left pec.

"Why haven't you asked me about them?" he asks, his voice rough and quiet.

"What?" She lifts her head, resting her chin on his chest.

"My scars," he replies. "Why haven't you asked me about them? Aren't you curious?"

Kaia's heart skips a beat. Should she be honest with him? She figures he'll know if she's lying, but she doesn't want to offend him.

As if he can read her mind, he says, "Tell me the truth."

He watches her with an intensity that she's not used to, and it makes her shift a little beneath the sheets.

"Yes, I'm curious," she replies, not wanting to expound upon her curiosity without being prompted.

"Then why haven't you asked?"

Kaia shrugs. "I got the feeling that it was something you were self-conscious about, and the last thing I wanted to do was gawk at them, or treat them like they were some kind of exhibit. I didn't want to make you uncomfortable."

Kaia didn't even realize his muscles had stiffened beneath her until she felt him relax.

"Did I say something wrong?"

Jason shakes his head, then leans in and presses a kiss against the top of Kaia's head. "No. You didn't."

"Then what-"

"You're the first person who's acted like they weren't there. I just wondered why."

Kaia blanches. "Have women actually gawked at you?"

"Not exactly. But they have…examined them the first time they've seen them."

Kaia feels anger rising up inside of her, unbidden. "No one deserves to be *examined*. No wonder you only had one-night stands." She cringes when she says the words, even though she hears Jason laugh. "I'm sorry, I didn't mean that."

"It's okay," he says, sliding his fingertips up and down Kaia's upper arm. "I haven't only had one-night stands, though," he admits.

Kaia's eyebrows draw together. "You haven't? I thought-"

"There was one woman," he admits carefully. "My last year in college, before I moved here. It wasn't serious, but it's probably as close to serious as I've ever allowed myself to get." His whole expression softens. "Before this."

"What happened?" Kaia asks immediately, her curiosity getting the better of her. Whatever it was that happened, it clearly still weighs heavily on Jason's mind, so Kaia quickly amends her question with, "You don't have to answer that if you don't want to."

Jason considers that for a moment.

"I don't want to get too deep into it, but she was curious about the scars, and when I told her the story behind them, she...she didn't take it well."

"That's terrible. Was it..."

"Was it what?"

Kaia bites her lip, considers for a moment whether or not she should voice this particular question. She decides to risk it, mostly because she's too curious not to.

"Was it somehow your fault?" That's the only way Kaia can imagine someone getting upset over scars that look like his, because otherwise, how could you possibly blame someone for something that happened that ended up with their chest and back being riddled with scars?

Kaia actually hears Jason swallow in the quiet that stretches between them. Hesitation flits across his handsome face for just a moment before he shakes his head. "No, it wasn't my fault."

Kaia reaches over and cups his face, planting a soft kiss on his lips. "I'm sorry you told that story to someone who didn't deserve to hear it."

"Me too," he replies, giving her a small smile.

"It's scary to let people see the parts of yourself that you want to keep hidden. When you do that with a person who ends up not being who you thought they were, that makes you want to keep them all locked up for good."

With an unreadable look on his face, Jason kisses her, long and lingering. "What about you?"

"My locked up parts?"

The corner of Jason's mouth cocks up. "Yeah. Still under heavy duty lock and key?"

Kaia grins at him. "I don't have anything like this," she says, sliding her hand across his chest. "Seems silly in comparison."

"Nothing about you is silly."

"I had a great home life growing up, and I managed to go off to college without any major traumas. I've just had a few bad relationships and even worse breakups. My hangups are silly."

"Bad relationships?" Jason asks, curious. He props himself up, a serious look in his eyes. "No one laid a hand on you, did they?"

"No," Kaia replies quickly. "No, nothing like that. I mean bad as in dating a deadbeat kind of way. Men—or, *boys* I should say—who made it clear that they didn't think I was anything special. It did a number on me for a while."

Jason slides his fingers through Kaia's hair, then tilts her head up and kisses her. "I think you're something special."

His voice is solemn and deep, and Kaia believes what he's telling her. In fact, he's made her feel this way ever since she ran into him on the sidewalk outside of his building, and she realizes this is probably one of the reasons she's been so drawn to him since that morning.

The realization hits her hard, right in the chest.

"Thank you." She nuzzles up against Jason's side, resting her head on his chest, and traces another one of his scars.

"Did you want to tell me about them? Is that why you asked?" Again, she doesn't want to push. But she's incredibly hopeful that they've reached the point in their relationship or, whatever it is, that he's willing to open up to her about them.

"No," he says, his gaze intense.

Kaia feels a flush of embarrassment heating her cheeks. "Oh, I-"

Before she can finish her sentence, Jason crooks his fingers beneath her chin, and tilts her head up so she's looking at him.

"Not yet. But soon," he says. "Someday soon, I think."

Kaia presses a kiss to the center of his chest, right above a knotted slash of scar tissue. "Whenever you're ready."

The air is thick with something that Kaia can't quite name, and she's desperate to break it up.

"I think they're beautiful, for what it's worth," she says, not exactly sure what makes her say that, of all things. She props herself up on her arm, and traces her finger along the silvery skin of another scar, following the length of it across his flesh. "You survived. You lived. And look what you've done with your life. You didn't let anything stop you, and that's…it's so brave, Jason. You're gorgeous. All of you."

Jason smiles. It's one Kaia hasn't ever seen before, one that's so beautiful in its intensity that it makes her breath catch.

Jason leans down and claims her lips with his. The kiss is searing and intense, and Kaia slings her leg over his hips until she's straddling him, his cock hard and ready, right where she needs him.

Jason grips Kaia's hips to keep her still, his fingers pressing into her skin.

"*You're* gorgeous," he whispers, his hands sliding up to cup her breasts. His thumbs graze across her nipples, puckering the skin there, and Jason pushes himself up so he can take one in his mouth, then the other. "You're so fucking gorgeous."

Kaia thinks her heart might beat out of her chest just hearing those words from him. A compliment like that from a man like him, well…it sure gives a girl's ego a boost.

"I want you to be mine," he continues, kissing his way across the valley between her breasts, his stubble scratching her sensitive skin. "I don't want anyone else to have you."

"I'm yours," she says. It's not exactly the kind of relationship confirmation she was looking for, but in the heat of the moment, she'll take it.

"You're mine," he repeats, a desperate look in his eyes.

"I'm yours."

With that, Jason angles his hips and thrusts up, and Kaia closes her eyes against the sweet stretch as he fills her.

"Oh, *fuck*." Jason wraps his arms around Kaia's waist, and buries his face in the crook of her neck. "You feel so perfect, so..."

Kaia slides her fingers through his hair, and lets him savor the moment. Before long, Jason tightens his hold on Kaia's hips, rocking her back and forth as he laves and sucks on her neck. She's holding onto him tight, desperately chasing the sparks of pleasure she feels every time she rocks.

"Lean back," Jason says, his lips brushing the shell of her ear. "I want to see."

Kaia pulls away from him, taking in his heavy lidded and lust-addled eyes as his gaze falls to her breasts. She'll do anything he asks her to when he looks at her like that.

She balances her weight on her knees. Jason lightly grips her upper arms as she moves backwards, not really sure what exactly it is that he wants her to do. He motions for her to plant her hands on the mattress, on either side of his calves, then he gently tugs on her calves until she's leveraging her weight on her feet. She feels a little ridiculous, like she's in some weird game of Twister, until she sees Jason's face, and she understands.

He wants to watch as he fucks her.

"I've got you," he says, reaching out to steady her hips as she starts moving. His eyes are focused on where his cock is sliding in and out of her. He's not getting as deep as he was in their previous position, but the eroticism of it all kicks up Kaia's arousal about another ten notches.

"You look so fucking gorgeous like this," Jason says. "You feel amazing."

Kaia rotates her hips on a downward thrust, making Jason's head fall back, and his mouth part as he takes in shallow breaths. Wanting to do any and everything she can to keep making him look like *that*, she lifts herself up, then slowly lowers herself down onto him, circling her hips when he fills her completely. He's letting out these little grunts as she moves faster, faster. She's chasing her own orgasm too, so, *so* close.

Like he knows that she needs something to help get her there, Jason drags the pad of his thumb across his tongue, then rubs maddening circles across Kaia's sensitive clit.

Just like that, she's coming.

Jason gathers her up into his arms, holding on tight as she rides out the waves of her powerful orgasm, breathing erratically against his neck. He gives her a minute to come down, then he's kissing her frantically as he flips them over, her back pressed into the soft mattress as he pumps his hips, driving into her at a relentless pace.

Jason takes Kaia's hands and twines their fingers together, as he stares down at her with an intensity in his eyes that *thrills* her. There's sweat beading above his brow, and she wraps her legs around his waist, pressing her heels against his ass as he comes with a shout, dragging her along with him into another orgasm.

Kaia loves feeling the weight of him on top of her as his breathing slowly returns to normal. She slides her fingertips up and down the curve of his spine, as he presses soft kisses on her neck.

"You're mine," he says, over and over again.

"I'm yours."

Chapter
14

"Don't take this the wrong way, because it's an observation, not a criticism. But you've gone completely off the grid lately," Chase says.

Jason watches the numbers in the elevator go higher and higher as it makes the climb to Chase's floor.

"I've been busy," Jason replies. "I asked if you wanted to grab a cup of coffee before this meeting, didn't I?"

Chase laughs. "Yeah. I bet it was tough for you to carve that fifteen minutes out of your busy schedule."

Jason just gives him a withering look, not really sure what there is to say, because it's true. He has gone off the grid. Time he used to spend with Chase on the nightclub scene looking for some fun followed by a one-night-stand is now mostly dedicated to Kaia.

"I'm doing something a little bit different now."

"I know," Chase replies, nodding. "And you seem happy."

"I am." Jason takes a long draw from his to-go cup.

"Am I going to get to meet her some day?"

Jason tenses at that, remembering the conversation he had with Kaia, where she made it quite clear that she didn't want their relationship to be some big secret. That she wouldn't allow it. And Jason doesn't want that, but he's not sure how to let go of his need to protect her by keeping her hidden away. Chase poses absolutely no threat to her. Jason knows this, and still…

"You've got to stop doing this to yourself, man."

"Doing what?"

Chase rolls his eyes. "Worrying that your past is going to come back to haunt you. That isn't going to happen."

"You don't know that," Jason replies angrily through his clenched teeth. "If you had any idea what it was like-"

Chase holds his hands up in surrender. "I was there afterwards, remember? You still haven't told her yet, have you?"

Jason presses his lips together, and looks up at the ceiling of the elevator. It's not moving fast enough.

"I'm not trying to tell you how to handle your relationships-"

"Really? Because it seems like that's exactly what you're doing."

The elevator comes to a halt, and the doors open. Two older men in suits walk in, and the air crackles with tension between Jason and his friend.

When they reach Chase's floor, Jason follows him to his office. They still have another fifteen minutes before their meeting starts, and Jason would prefer to have this conversation over and done with before that. Even though there isn't much that could throw Jason off of his game, he doesn't want this hanging between them when they're trying to talk to the board of Chase's company about long-term investments.

Chase stops when they reach his assistant's desk. Amber is a pretty, auburn-haired woman with bright blue eyes and a smattering of freckles across her nose. They give her a girl-next-door sun kissed look that goes a long way toward making you forget that she's a total spitfire, and someone who can wind up his friend in a way that no other woman can.

"There were coffees waiting for us at the shop downstairs," he tells her, holding his cup out for her to see.

Amber doesn't even look up from the spreadsheet she's working on. "I know."

"There was one for Jason, too."

"I know. Good morning, Jason."

"Morning, Amber," Jason replies with a grin.

"How did you know Jason and I were getting coffee this morning? I didn't put that on my calendar."

A slow smile spreads across Amber's face. "That's what you pay me the big bucks for." She looks up at her boss, her eyebrows drawn together. "Oh, wait. You actually don't pay me the big bucks. But you should. Right, Jason?"

Jason can actually see his friend's shoulders stiffen. "I'd

pay you the big bucks if you could somehow manage to get the numbers for the Morgan account on my desk before this meeting in..." He stretches out his arm and looks at his watch. "Ten minutes. Randall was here till two trying to undo that mess."

"I'd like to remind you that there's a witness here. Jason, you heard that, right?"

"I certainly did."

"No way," Chase replies, as he makes his way into his office.

"Way," Amber whispers to Jason, which makes him laugh.

Jason takes a few steps forward into Chase's office, where his friend is standing behind his desk, staring down at the open folder in his hands with wide eyes.

"Holy shit," he whispers. "She's not real."

"I'm very real," Amber yells from her desk. "And I'm holding you to your promise."

"I didn't promise anything."

"Jason, he promised, didn't he?" Amber replies sweetly. "Loads of cash."

"He did." Jason lets out a short huff of a laugh before he takes a swig of his coffee.

Irritated, Chase closes the folder in his hands and puts it down on his desk. "Where are the-"

"In the purple folder."

"She doesn't even know what I'm going to ask for," he mumbles.

"Yes I do, and it's in the purple folder."

Chase opens the purple folder, and by the tense set of his shoulders, Jason knows that's exactly what he was going to ask Amber for.

"Shut the door," Chase grumbles.

Jason turns and winks at a grinning, triumphant Amber as he does as his friend asks.

"*You're* lecturing *me* about my love life while you've got *that* going on?"

Chase narrows his eyes. "Got what going on?"

"Whatever it is that's going on between you two."

"There's nothing going on between us," Chase says.

"Whatever you say."

"Besides," Chase replies. "We weren't talking about me, we were talking about you."

"No, *you* were talking about me. I was avoiding talking about it at all."

"Look." Chase leans forward, resting his hands on his desk. "You're my oldest friend, and I love you like a brother."

"I don't like where this is going." Jason sighs.

"No good is going to come of keeping that secret from her."

Jason scrubs his hand over his face, his fingertips sliding across his raspy cheeks. "I'll tell her when I'm ready."

"History isn't going to repeat itself, man."

"You don't know that, and I'm not taking any chances."

"What do you mean you're not taking any chances?"

Jason presses his lips together, not wanting to answer, because he knows his friend won't approve.

"Christ, you have a security detail on her, don't you?"

Jason's silence is all the answer Chase needs. "And she doesn't know?"

"I'll tell her when I'm ready."

Chase shakes his head, with an unreadable look clouding his eyes. "This is all going to blow up in your face, you know that, right?"

"I've got it under control."

Chapter 15

Jason and Kaia are curled up on his incredibly large, ridiculously comfortable sofa. Jason has his feet propped up on his coffee table, and Kaia's legs are flung over his thighs, making it easier for her to curl against his side. Her head is resting on his shoulder, arm wrapped across his chest. She's nuzzling his neck, feeling the familiar rasp of his stubble against her forehead as she breathes in the clean, spicy scent of him.

They're both fully clothed, and there's not the heady rush of need pulsing through their veins. It's just a normal night together, with half-full glasses of wine on the end table beside them, and the two of them wrapped up in each other's arms.

It's perfect.

"Do you have any plans on Saturday evening?" Jason asks.

Kaia isn't sure how long it's been since either of them has

said anything, and it startles her.

"Actually," she says hesitantly, sliding her hand across the soft fabric of Jason's shirt. "I might."

If Kaia wasn't so attuned to Jason, she would miss the way his muscles tighten ever-so-slightly at her response.

"Yeah? You do?"

Now that she thinks about it, this is the first time since they started seeing each other that she's actually had plans when he asks her out. Maybe he's wondering if she's teasing?

"I do." She doesn't know if she should rush to tell him what those plans are, or if she should wait for him to ask. "Were you…did you have something in mind?"

"It's nothing," he says curtly.

"You were going to ask me to do nothing?"

Jason lets out a small, tense laugh, and shakes his head. "It's a fundraiser. It's a relatively small get together, but it'll be full of a lot of people I know. I'd like for you to come with me."

He took to heart that she didn't want their relationship to be a secret, so of course she'd have other plans on the night he wants to introduce her to some of his friends.

"A friend of mine from college has been working on a contract in Japan, and he's coming to town for his birthday. I haven't seen him since we graduated."

Jason tenses again. "It's fine."

Kaia reaches up and cups his face, turning his head until her lips touch his, softly, tenderly.

"You listened to what I wanted."

Jason pulls away, his brows furrowed. "What?"

Kaia laughs, then pulls her bottom lip between her teeth. "I told you that I didn't want our relationship to be some secret, and you listened."

He nods a little. "Of course. I told you it wasn't a secret. I just wasn't ready to let people know."

"For reasons that you didn't want to tell me about. And now you are? Ready to let people know?"

Jason takes a deep breath. "I'm ready to take *this* step," he explains. "But if you don't want-"

"I want to go," Kaia replies quickly. "Did you think I was preemptively making up an excuse to tell you no or something?" She's not angry, just genuinely curious.

Jason shakes his head. "No. It's just the first time you've had other plans, so I wondered. That's all."

Kaia kisses him again, long and slow until she can feel his lips smiling against hers.

"A friend from college has been working on a contract project in Japan since graduation. He's coming back to the States to visit and we're all going out for his birthday, which is on Saturday."

With a deep inhale through his nostrils, Jason nods. "Okay."

"What time is the fundraiser?"

"It starts at eight," he explains.

"Is it okay if we're a little late? Don't you rich, high-society types consider lateness to be fashionable or something?"

Jason pulls her closer, pressing a kiss against the top of her head as he laughs. "You watch too much television."

"So, you're an incredibly punctual bunch, then? Got it."

"Not the most punctual, no."

"We can be late, then?"

"Yeah." He pulls her closer. "We can be late."

"Good. Then you've got a date."

"A beautiful date," he amends, pressing another kiss against her hair.

"Mmmm." Kaia tucks herself closer against his side.

"Tell me about your friend. You said it's a *he*?" Jason goes for nonchalant and a little teasing, but the hint of jealousy isn't lost on Kaia.

"It is a he," she tells him, reaching out and twining her fingers with his. "A he with a long-term girlfriend. A he that I'm not even remotely romantically or sexually attracted to."

"I wasn't-"

"Yes you were. You were fishing."

Jason laughs. "Okay, yes. I was fishing."

"I can't believe it."

"What? That I'd fish for information?"

Kaia sits up, and in a move that seems to take Jason off guard, she slings her leg over his hips until she's straddling him. "No, that you'd be…insecure enough to fish for information."

He narrows his eyes, and lets out a little growl as he grips Kaia's hips. "I'm not insecure," he says quickly. "Just curious."

"Anything you want to know, all you have to do is ask."

"I wanted to know who you were going out with, and you told me."

"Mmm-hmmm," Kaia hums teasingly.

"I'm not some caveman, Kaia. I don't feel threatened by you being friends with other men."

"Okay, good to know." She slides her fingers through his hair the way she knows he likes, and grinds down on him, making his eyelids flutter shut. "I told you, I'm yours."

He grips her hips tighter. "You're mine," he repeats.

"All yours. Now, whatever are you going to do with me?"

Jason slides his hands up her sides, until his thumbs caress the gentle swell of her breasts. "So many things," he whispers, before planting a kiss on her neck. "So. Many. Things."

Kaia's working on a design for a client with her laptop perched on the kitchen table, when Janine walks up behind her, and puts her hands over Kaia's eyes.

"How did this ever become a thing with our group of friends?" Kaia asks, reaching up and gently patting Janine's hands, so she'd remove them.

"I don't know, but it's still fun."

"Fun for you, maybe. Not so much for the person getting creeped up on."

Janine grins. "Yeah, that's the point." She places a bottle of Kaia's favorite juice on the table in front of her. "Long time no see, stranger."

Kaia takes a deep breath as she reaches for the juice, a guilty look on her face. "Sorry I haven't been around much. I've been really busy with a couple of new clients."

Janine gives her a look that indicates Kaia definitely needs to cut the shit. "Is 'busy with new clients' code for 'busy having sweaty rabbit sex with your hot, rich boyfriend?'"

Kaia scrunches up her nose. "We don't have sweaty rabbit sex."

"Oh, please. You can convince me of a LOT of stuff, Kaia, but you'll never be able to convince me of *that*."

Kaia gives her friend a sly grin. "Okay."

"I'm not being critical, just know that before you hear what I'm getting ready to say."

Kaia's breath catches in her throat, because Janine has never been one to pull punches, and Kaia has a pretty good idea of what she's getting ready to say. And the truth is, she can't deny it.

"Don't you think this is all moving a little fast? I'm all for love-at-first-sight-"

"We're not in love," Kaia objects. She can definitely see herself getting there. She's on the verge of it, really, if she lets herself think about it, but she's not there yet.

"Okay," Janine says patiently. "Still, you're with him so much I barely see you, Kaia. You're over there almost every night."

"I like being with him." She shrugs. There's really not anything more to it than that. "He makes me feel special,

Janine. You know it's been a long time since I've had that."

With a soft look in her eyes, Janine scoots her chair closer, and takes Kaia's hand. "I'm glad to hear it. And you deserve to have someone who treats you that way. I just want to make sure you're not losing sight of other things, that's all."

"I'm not, I promise."

"I got the text that you were going to go to some fundraiser with him on Saturday night, and I worried, that's all."

"I'm not skipping out on Clark's dinner, I promise. I'm going, I'm just going to go to this party after. He wants me to meet his friends; I told him that was something that was important to me, and I didn't want to turn him down when he made the effort."

What Kaia doesn't want to tell Janine is that Jason is so secretive about his past that she's scared to turn down this opportunity in fear that she won't get another one. He's ready to introduce her to his friends, and she wants to take him up on that offer.

"I understand." Janine squeezes Kaia's hand. "I'm just trying to look out for you. I don't want you…I don't want you losing yourself, that's all."

"I won't, I promise. I'm going to finish up this design, then I'm heading out to meet Clark for coffee since I'm cutting our time short on Saturday."

If nothing else, Janine looks pleased by that.

"Then, when I get back, maybe we can watch a movie?"

Janine gives her a warm smile. "That sounds great. I'm

gonna head out for a bit, maybe get some snacks?"

"Popcorn. And chocolate, lots of chocolate."

"You've got it," she says, as she stands up and slides her bag over her shoulder. "I'll see you later?"

"See you later."

Kaia finishes up the design she's working on and emails the proofs to her client. She changes out of her lounging-at-home clothes, and takes a taxi to the Upper West Side park where she and Clark agreed to meet.

She stands with her arms crossed over the top of a wrought iron fence, watching the way the sun glints on the water of the Hudson. When Clark hasn't shown up, she pulls her phone out of her back pocket, seeing she has a missed text.

Running late, sry. Be there soon.

She smiles when a few minutes later she feels Clark's hands covering her eyes, and she reaches up, squeezing his wrists.

"Hey, Richardson," he says warmly. She can hear the smile in his voice.

She turns to greet him, but freezes when she sees a man running straight for them. He tackles Clark to the ground, and Kaia only has a split second to process what's going on before two men flank her sides and pull her away, screaming.

Chapter 16

Jason's phone buzzes on the inside breast pocket of his blazer, in the middle of a very important meeting. When he sees the name of the head of Kaia's security detail pop up on his screen, his heart plummets all the way down to his stomach.

He stands and excuses himself immediately, claiming urgent business, and he practically runs to the hallway outside of the conference room he was seated in.

"Paul," he says frantically when he accepts the call, not even waiting for any kind of a greeting. "What's going on?"

Without wasting a second, Paul replies, "We have a situation here." His voice is maddeningly calm; it's such a stark contrast to the panic skittering across Jason's nerve endings that it makes him want to claw his own skin off.

"What kind of situation?"

There's a voice on the other end of the call—a voice that doesn't belong to Paul—and no matter how hard he tries, Jason cannot make out what the voice is saying.

"Hold on." Jason isn't sure if Paul is talking to him or the person who was just speaking, but he hears bits and pieces of their muffled conversation. The fact that he isn't getting the information he asked for *right the hell now* pisses him off.

"Paul? Paul!" he practically shouts, but…nothing.

If Jason is honest with himself, he's been expecting this call ever since he went to Kaia's apartment and told her he wanted to find out if the two of them could have more than just a one-night stand.

Jason knew then that he wouldn't be able to stay away from her, that the more he got of her the more he'd want. He knew that wanting more from her and taking it came with its own set of risks, and he'd planned for those risks.

Jason had the security team in place before he even went over to her apartment that night.

He'd briefed Paul and his guys on what he feared could happen to Kaia, what they might need to guard her against. He told them all the ways he'd dreamed up over the years that someone he loved could be taken from him.

All the ways that someone he loved could be used against him.

After all that planning and precaution, his worst fears still seemed to be coming to fruition.

He knew this would happen, but he wanted Kaia anyway.

Now…now he feels sick.

And he's running out of patience.

"God damn it, Paul. Talk to me!"

Paul knew better to ignore the growling, urgent voice of his employer.

"It's fine," he replies, a little breathless. "She's fine. We have her. We're just trying to smooth something over here. I'll call you right back."

With that, Paul ends the call.

What the hell does he have to smooth over? Without having anything to go on to tell him what exactly happened, knowing that Kaia is safe and in the hands of her perfectly capable security detail makes the panic calm just a bit.

It comes right back when it hits him that Kaia is safe in the hands of her perfectly capable security detail…that he never told her he'd hired. He'd been putting it off until the right moment (or so he was telling himself), and now the situation was completely out of his hands.

Chase was right. This is blowing up in his face.

Not wanting to wait for Paul to get back to him, he hits Kaia's speed dial on his phone, desperate to get control of things. To get out ahead of this before she's so angry and scared that he can't make things right.

He wants to make sure she's okay, and he needs to explain himself more than anything.

The phone rings and rings, then goes straight to her voicemail. All of his thoughts and feelings just trip their way out of his mouth.

"Kaia, it's me. Are you okay? I want to talk to you. I need to explain. I need to hear your voice. Please call me back."

He ends the call, then hits her speed dial again. He gets her voicemail. *Again.*

He starts typing out a text when his phone rings.

"It's Paul. Sorry for-"

"What in the hell happened?" Jason growls.

"We followed her to Riverside, where a caucasian male stepped up behind her and held his hands over her eyes. My guys reacted quickly, just like I trained them to," he explains, almost defensively. "They took the guy down, and got Kaia out of harm's way."

That sounded way less climactic than he'd been anticipating. "Okay, so…what's the situation?"

Jason is antsy. He needs more details, and he needs them immediately.

"The guy was a friend of hers. She was meeting him for coffee."

Jason's stomach plummets. Of all the scenarios he'd conjured up in his head about why Paul and his team would need to spring into action, he'd never considered this one.

"Is he all right?"

"Just a little banged up," Paul says. "My guys weren't too hard on him, but I think it might be a good idea to get a lawyer down here, just in case. We've gotten him calmed down, but I think it would be a good precaution just in case he decides he wants to involve the legal system here."

Jason takes a deep breath, trying to steady his racing heart. "Okay, I'll send one down there. Is Kaia around?"

There's a long pause before Paul says, "Yes."

"She didn't answer when I called her earlier. Pass the phone over so I can talk to her."

Paul clears his throat, and what follows is an uncomfortable silence that seems like it lasts an eternity.

"Just do it," Jason commands.

"I had to explain to her who we were, and who hired us," Paul explains reluctantly. "I had to give her the bare minimum in order to keep her from making a scene."

Reaching up and pinching the bridge of his nose, Jason lets out an unsteady breath. After a turn of events that he never could have anticipated, he's really kicking himself for not being up front with her before all of this happened. He hired men to keep her safe, men she had no clue even existed. And in his unrelenting desire to protect her, he wound up scaring the hell out of her.

He can't imagine how she's feeling. He wants to know. He wants to *talk* to her.

"Let me talk to her," Jason commands. There's another stretch of silence, and Jason is very quickly losing his patience. "Get her on the goddamn phone, Paul."

"She doesn't want to talk to you. She was...she's pretty adamant about that."

Fuck. Even though he doesn't blame Kaia for being angry

and upset, he can't let this fester. He has to explain things to her before it's too late.

He just hopes it's not already too late.

Jason slides the phone back into his pocket, and makes his way back into the conference room, where the meeting has continued on in his absence. When he walks in, the chatter stops, and everyone looks in his direction.

"We're going to have to cut this short," Jason says, with barely suppressed irritation in his voice. "There's an emergency I have to attend to." He doesn't wait for anyone to respond, he just turns and leaves.

He had always been concerned about a relationship getting in the way of business, but now that it's happened, he doesn't *care.* All he can think about is getting to Kaia. Maybe that should scare him, given that most of his life is about is work, but it doesn't.

Instead, a strange new feeling hits him square in his chest. It's not the end of the world. The meeting he just canceled can and will be rescheduled. He can trust the people in his employ to deal with anything pressing in his absence. Everything else can wait until tomorrow.

The world won't stop spinning if he takes a little breather to make things right with his girlfriend.

This kind of thing won't happen every day, but it's okay for him to take half a day for himself every once in a while.

He's just hoping Kaia will hear him out.

Chapter 17

"Wait, wait," Janine says, as she dips her spoon into the fresh pint of ice cream that Kaia brought home from the bodega around the corner. "I'm not sure I'm hearing you correctly. He had people *following* you?"

"A 'security detail,'" she says, obnoxiously using air quotes. "A security detail that I didn't know about, so...stalkers, maybe? I don't know what they are in this particular situation." Stalkers seems an appropriate name for a bunch of guys she didn't know following her every move.

Kaia digs out a chunk of chocolate chip cookie dough, then pops it into her mouth. She was shaking with anger when she left the park this afternoon, after everything had settled between Clark and the security guys who accosted him. She needed something to occupy her mind, and picking up something that was sure to give her a sugar rush seemed like a really good idea.

As the sweet ice cream slid across her tongue, she was glad she made that decision earlier.

Janine narrows her eyes. "A security detail for *what*?"

"I don't know," Kaia replies with a shrug.

"Isn't that the very first question you asked him?"

Kaia sighs. "It's probably the first question I would've asked him if I had actually spoken to him."

"What?" Janine asks incredulously. "You haven't even spoken to him?"

"After everything happened, I was busy dealing with Clark and trying to get him to calm down. And I knew that if I talked to Jason while I was angry, I was going to wind up saying something that I could never take back. Angry as I am at him, I'm not sure that's how I want to end things." She leans forward to get another scoop of ice cream. "Or *if* I want to end things."

That was the crux of the emotional turmoil she was feeling. She felt like this should be a deal breaker, but she wasn't sure if she wanted it to be one.

Either way, it seems like Janine understands where she's coming from. If not, she's doing a good job of pretending.

"It's better to give yourself some time to process, rather than making a rash decision you might regret later."

"Yeah," Kaia replies absentmindedly.

"Is Clark okay?"

Kai nods. "He is. He got a few scrapes, but he wasn't hurt.

He was more angry than anything."

"Rightfully so." Janine slides the back of her spoon across her tongue, licking off the remaining ice cream.

"Right? He comes to meet me thinking we're going to go for coffee and catch up, and then out of nowhere he gets tackled in the middle of a park."

Just recounting the events of the day makes a fresh wave of anger course through Kia's veins. How could Jason do this without telling her? She knew he had his secrets that he'd share with her in due time, but she never thought he'd hire security for her without telling her what was going on.

Is her life in danger? Is he just being cautious? Does it have something to do with his scars? These are all questions she both wants and needs answers to, she's just not ready to ask them yet.

Like Janine is reading her mind, she asks, "Any idea why he did this? I mean, he's a businessman…is it a front for the mafia or something? Or is he just one of those paranoid types?"

Kaia wants to tell Janine that she's being ridiculous. The mafia? Really? But the truth is, she doesn't *know* if Janine is being ridiculous.

For all she knows, Jason's reluctance to share with her could have everything to do with not wanting her to get involved in whatever it is that he has going on. She's realizing now that she hardly knows the man she's been sleeping with and…well, falling in love with.

She's falling in love with Jason, and what happened this

afternoon put a screeching stop to the whole thing.

"He's not one of those paranoid types." That she knows.

"You *are* going to talk to him, though, right? You said you weren't sure if you wanted to end things, but…you're going to give him a chance to explain himself first, aren't you?"

"Why are you looking at me like that?"

Janine shrugs. "I'm not looking at you like anything."

"Yes you are. You want to say something, but you're wondering if you should. Just say it; I'm not going to get upset."

Janine takes a deep breath. "I know how you feel about him. I've spent a grand total of five minutes with the two of you, and there's something electric between you when you're around each other. I know you, and I just can't imagine that no matter how angry you are now, that you'll be able to walk away without finding out why he did what he did."

Just to play devil's advocate, Kaia asks, "Does the why really matter?"

With a smirk, Janine replies, "Of course it does. You of all people should know that."

"What's that supposed to mean?"

Janine puts her spoon down, and sits up, giving Kaia her full attention. "For as long as I've known you, you're always the one trying to get me to see the other side of my anger. Like, perfect example: remember when I first started seeing Charlie, and we saw him with that redhead at the movies?"

"The redhead who wound up being his stepsister?" Kaia asks, amused.

"Yeah, that one." Janine lets out a little laugh. "I was ready to write him off after just seeing the two of them sitting next to each other in a movie theater. I would have, too, if you hadn't talked me into getting the whole story."

Kaia gets where she's coming from, but, "Seeing your new boyfriend at the movies with some other woman is different than finding out that your new boyfriend is *having you followed without your knowledge.*"

Janine playfully rolls her eyes.

"What?!"

"I'm not trying to make excuses for the guy, but having you *followed* and hiring a security detail for you are two very different things."

Kaia shakes her head. "Not when you're the person being followed. Not when you didn't know."

"But one indicates spying, Kaia. The other indicates that he just wants you to be safe."

"Safe from *what,* is the thing. If there's something I need to be kept safe from, shouldn't he be telling me that?"

Janine looks at Kaia like she's lost her mind. "Kaia, he's a quadrillionaire. Who knows who would come after you because of your connection to him. Seems to me the explanation could be as simple as him taking a precaution."

Kaia takes a moment and lets that marinate. Her eyelids flutter shut, and she thinks about the scars that mark Jason's gorgeous body. For a moment, she's able to put herself in his shoes, understanding how terrible it must be to live his life in that kind of fear. It actually breaks Kaia's heart a little, and she's wondering if this fear is a holdover from whatever it is that he went through that gave him those scars, or if there's someone out there that she needs to be afraid of.

"He's not just taking precautions," she says.

"You won't know for sure unless you talk to him, Kaia."

She does know it. She knows it in her bones, and that's what scares the hell out of her, and makes the idea of talking to him about this so damned scary. Before finding out about the security, she thought that whatever it was that kept him from entering into relationships, what kept him from taking her out on dates in public, what left him with those scars… she thought it was something that was still lodged firmly in his past.

Now, she knows that whatever it is, it's in the present. And with her in his life, she's going to have to deal with those demons, too.

She just isn't sure she's ready to do that.

Chapter 18

J ason's car pulls down Kaia's street, and he feels a rush of
nervous adrenaline when he sees someone sitting on the
front steps of her building.

Disappointment settles bitterly in his stomach when the
car gets closer and he realizes that it isn't her, but her roommate.

When the car comes to a stop, Jason opens the door, not
bothering to wait for his driver to do it. He can feel the weight
of her gaze on him as he stands. He's only met her once for five
minutes; he isn't even sure if she remembers who he is.

He's heard a lot about her from Kaia; he probably knows
more about Janine than he does some people he's actually
spent a considerable amount of time with. But he can't assume
she's told Janine as much about him.

The second he sees the look on Janine's face—a mixture
of barely restrained judgment and surprise—he knows that

she does remember him. And that Kaia told her about what happened this afternoon.

He shifts uncomfortably. Jason is a man of wealth and power, and part of establishing that power in any interaction is being prepared for all possible scenarios. He never lets anyone catch him off guard.

But his wealth of business knowledge and negotiating tactics can't prepare him for how to deal with the angry best friend of the woman he's falling in love with.

Since he's never allowed himself a relationship, he isn't sure how to deal when one hits a rocky patch. He also isn't all that familiar with apologizing or admitting he was wrong, but he needs to do that, too.

He decides that instead of going with his first instinct— offering Janine a polite smile as he walks past (assuming she'll let him walk past)—he's going to sit down and talk to her. Maybe she can offer him some insight into the situation that will do him some good. He figures it's better than barreling into the situation without getting a read on it. Janine knows better than anyone how Kaia's feeling, especially since she wouldn't answer any of Jason's calls.

"Hey," she says warily as he approaches her.

Jason notices the lit cigarette in her hand. It's almost down to the filter; clearly she's been sitting out here for a while.

He takes a seat next to her, feeling the cool concrete on the backs of his legs.

"Hey," he replies.

"Don't tell Kaia," she says, holding the cigarette between her index finger and thumb before she stomps the butt out on the step beside her. "She thinks I quit. And I have, for the most part. It's just that some days, I really...well, it helps."

Jason nods, resting his elbows on his knees. "I won't say anything," he replies, adding a quiet, "Seems I'm pretty good at keeping secrets." He figures it's best to go ahead and address the elephant in the room.

Janine nods. "You know, I've heard about that."

Jason isn't at all surprised. He's guessing that spending all afternoon consoling an angry Kaia might be one of the reasons why she's sitting out here taking a smoke break.

"I'm going to be better about that. If she'll let me."

Janine nods slowly. "I think she might be willing to do that." Hope swells in Jason's chest, but it's quickly deflated when Janine follows that up with, "Eventually."

He didn't expect to come here and have everything forgiven. He expected a difficult path, one where he'd have to lay himself bare to make her understand where he was coming from. Still, hearing the word "eventually" is a little discouraging.

"I've been keeping secrets for a long time," he explains. "This whole relationship thing is incredibly new to me, but...I'm trying not to keep the secrets anymore.

Janine nods in what seems like understanding. "That's a good way to be, but I think it might be a little too late in this particular situation."

Jason takes a long, deep breath, and then lets out a bitter laugh. "So it seems."

"It's not my place to say this, really. I want you to understand that I'm speaking out of turn before you hear what I have to say next. It's just that I haven't seen Kaia this happy in a really long time. And I don't think you're a bad guy - I'm pretty good at reading people, and that's not the vibe I'm getting here at all."

Jason isn't quite sure where this is going, but he'd like to get there as soon as possible. "So what is this thing that isn't your place to say?"

Janine lowers her hands, and plants her palms on the steps before she leans back. "Your relationship isn't my business. But Kaia and her happiness *are* my business, and...god, you really should've said something to her about this before she found out the way that she did. She thinks you were having her followed."

Jason blanches in irritation at himself. Yet another thing he hadn't counted on when he decided to bring on a security team without telling her: that she'd find out about it and get the wrong idea.

"I would *never* do that."

Janine shrugs. "Based on her reaction, it doesn't seem like she knows you well enough to believe that."

True as it may be, that's certainly not something that he wanted to hear. "I've been alone for a long time," he explains, not quite sure why he feels compelled to do it in the first place.

"I'm not in the habit of informing people about my decisions."

"No offense," she says, "but I get the feeling that even if you were, this isn't a decision that you would've shared with Kaia."

He doesn't have a response for that, because she is absolutely correct.

"I get that it must be scary for you, letting someone like Kaia be attached to you publicly. She's amazing, and people are assholes when it comes to strangers in the spotlight. And who knows what some loon might do in order to get to someone like you?"

Jason's breath nearly catches in his throat. If Janine, someone who is pretty far removed from his situation can understand that that's a worry for him, surely he'll be able to open Kaia's eyes and make her understand, too?

Janine isn't finished making her point, though.

"You have to give her all the facts here, Jason."

He knows that. He knows how unfair it is to ask Kaia to commit to him when she doesn't even know what she's committing to: a life of luxury, where she'll never want for anything, but a life that could be taken away, threatened, or changed in the blink of an eye.

It happened to him and his parents when he was younger, and he's been terrified of history repeating itself ever since. So terrified that he was willing to live the rest of his life off on one-night stands and the loneliness that followed them.

Now, he wants more.

He wants *Kaia*.

He knows that having her in his life means sharing all the shattered pieces of himself that he's always been afraid of letting anyone see. It means taking the risk knowing that she might not want anything to do with him one she sees those pieces.

Truthfully, he's scared. It's a difficult thing for someone like Jason to admit to. But what scares him more is the thought of losing Kaia because he didn't let her in, and always wondering what might've been if he was willing to take that leap.

"Do you think she'd slam the door in my face if I went upstairs and knocked?"

Janine shrugs. "There's only one way to find that out, I guess."

Jason stands, and holds out his hand. Janine takes it, and gives it a squeeze.

"Thank you," he says. "For the insight, and for being there for her when I let her down."

Janine seems almost taken aback by that, and tilts her head, like she's seeing him in a different light. He hopes like hell she is. It gives him hope that Kaia might forgive him.

"You're welcome," she replies, a friendly smile on her face. "I'll give you guys some time."

Jason grins as he makes his way up the steps. "I appreciate that."

"One more thing?"

He turns. "What's that?"

"If you hurt her, or if I come home one day and find out that you've lied to her, or kept something else from her, I will kill you."

Despite the threat, Jason can't help but smile. "Fair enough."

With his heart feeling like it's about to beat right out of his chest, Jason reaches up and raps on Kaia's front door. He hears footsteps, and through the thick wooden door, he makes out, "Did you forget your key again?"

The last word trails off as he sees the peephole darken. Since she knows he's the one standing on the other side of the door, he's a little stunned when she actually opens it. If she's surprised to see him there, she doesn't show it. Her face is well-schooled to the point of indifference.

It's not the most welcoming sight Jason's ever seen, even though she's still as beautiful as she's ever been. Her eyebrows slowly draw together, and when she looks at him with anger in her eyes, it makes Jason wish for the indifference she'd shown him only moments before.

"Did the fact that I wouldn't answer your calls, and telling Paul that I didn't want to talk to you not make it explicitly clear that I don't, in fact, want to talk to you?"

"Kaia," he pleads. "Please let me explain."

"Why do you want to explain now? Seems to me the best time to explain would've been before you hired a group of men to follow me around and spy on me night and day."

She's *livid*. He expected that she would be, and he understands why she is. But he's not sure how to talk her down. He holds his hands out, palms open in surrender. "I didn't...that's not what happened. Please, Kaia. Will you let me explain?"

Kaia inhales, long and deep, then folds her arms across her chest. Jason can see that it's working, can see her defenses falling little by little. The businessman in him is oh-so-tempted to use that to his advantage, but he doesn't want to pressure her. He's toeing such a delicate line, and one wrong move either way could make everything crumble. As desperate as he is for Kaia to hear him out, he knows that it has to be on her terms.

So far, everything has been on his terms, and judging by the state of things between them, that hasn't worked out so well so far.

"Not tonight," she says.

It's not a no, but it's not a definite enough answer for him to feel good about walking away from her tonight.

"Tomorrow, maybe?" he suggests hopefully.

She looks so vulnerable right now; he finds himself reaching out for her without thinking about it, wanting to take her hands in his. He wants to give them a gentle pull and hold her close. He fights that desire with every fiber of his being.

"I'd like it if you came over to my place, so we can have some privacy. And I promise you that whatever you want to know, I'll tell you."

He's offering her everything. Every single thing that he's kept hidden for most of his life, and it's terrifying. But they are the words she was looking for, he can tell by the way she relaxes.

"Anything?"

Jason nods solemnly. "Anything. I promise you." He's not sure what his promise means to her, but he hopes like hell it's something.

A few never-ending, heart-stopping moments pass, and she finally breaks the silence with a reluctant, "Okay."

He almost can't believe what he's hearing, and is completely unable to hide the utter relief in his voice when he says, "Okay?"

He's surprised, and hopeful.

"Yes," she says, and the corners of her beautiful mouth tilt up into something that looks kind of like a smile. "Okay."

Chapter 19

Kaia is so nervous throughout the day that she hardly gets any work done. It isn't until she's drawn and redrawn the same section of the design she's working on several times over that she decides that she's going to call it quits for the day.

She can't get any work done when she's distracted thinking about what tonight will bring.

Kaia doesn't know if she's still angry at Jason, or relieved that he's willing to tell her anything about him that she wants to know. It's probably a mix of the two, which is making things even more complicated for her than they should be.

She doesn't like that the only reason she found out about Jason's secret security detail was because they tackled Clark in the park. Would he have ever told her otherwise? It bothers her to think how long that could've gone on without her knowing.

Before Jason left her apartment last night, he'd practically begged Kaia to agree to let the security team stand guard overnight, until he could explain to her why he'd hired them in the first place. Since he could've ordered them to watch her without her being the wiser, Kaia thinks it's a good sign that he asked for her approval anyway.

That's what makes her give it to him.

Jason telling her that he's ready to open up to her about anything goes a long way toward quelling some of the anger she feels toward him. She's not sure what the outcome of tonight's discussion is going to be, but she feels significantly better about the way it's going to go than she did yesterday, so that's something.

Yesterday, Kaia thought she was done with Jason. All she wanted was to go back to her life before she met Jason. A life where she could meet a friend in the park without worrying about him being taken for a threat and accosted.

Today, Kaia is full of anticipation. She realizes that's probably foolish, but she can't help herself. She's never wanted to pressure him into talking about his past if he's not ready, and she's still not going to pressure him. Once she gets to his place, she'll see how things go. If she thinks he's going to be comfortable talking about something, then she'll ask him about it.

She just hopes like hell he's actually going to follow through with his promise to tell her anything she wants to know.

If Kaia's honest with herself, there's a part of her that

worries that maybe he told her he's ready to open up to her just to get her to agree to come over. That maybe he thinks once they're alone together again, he'll be able to get her back into bed, and so swept up in him that she forgets about what made her angry with him in the first place.

Kaia decides not to let those thoughts fester, because they can't lead to anything good. Jason seems to be making an effort, and she's going to believe that he's being honest with her. Otherwise, she's setting them up for failure before she even walks through his front door.

She watches the clock as it crawls toward 8PM. Jason told her he'd send his driver over to pick her up, and he's right on time, pulling up in front of her building at 7:40 on the dot.

On the short ride over to Jason's, Kaia second-guesses her choice in clothing. She didn't want to get too dressed up, didn't want to make Jason think that sex was an option tonight. She wonders if maybe she went too casual, deciding on jeans and a sweater. As the car weaves through traffic, she almost laughs at how silly it is that she's worried about the outfit she decided to wear when her boyfriend bares his soul to her.

When the driver opens her door in front of Jason's apartment building, she recognizes one of the men she'd seen in the park the other day; one of the guys who helped smooth things over with Clark after he'd been tackled. This man—whose name she doesn't know—is standing in the lobby in plain view, giving her a tight smile and a short nod.

Kaia has never seen this man in all the times she's been

over here. In fact, she's never seen anyone in this lobby other than the doorman and the concierge, and the occasional resident on their way out the door.

It's a small thing, but she loves that something that Jason had hidden is now out in the open.

Kaia figures that probably bodes well for tonight.

Kaia and Jason sit on either side of his sofa, the width of the middle cushion between them. It's a strange feeling, being so distant, and so different from all the other times she's been over here. Times when the two of them would curl up against each other, unable to keep their hands to themselves. Hell, half of the time they'd forego the living room altogether, and Jason would walk her back to the bedroom, hand-in-hand, desperate to worship her body.

Kaia shakes away those thoughts. Tonight isn't about sex.

"Thank you for coming," Jason says.

"Of course. I...I wanted to hear you out."

They're both completely tense, like a couple of strangers. The contrast between how things are between them now, and how they used to be hits Kaia hard.

"I want to start by apologizing to you," Jason says.

Kaia thinks he's going to follow up with something, but the words just hang there between them.

"Apologize for what?" Kaia doesn't want a blanket apology. She wants Jason to list all the things he's sorry for so that she can make sure they're both on the same page about what is and is not acceptable between them.

"For not telling you about the security. I'm not sorry for hiring them," he clarifies. "I'll explain to you why. But I am sorry for keeping it from you, and sorry that you found out the way that you did. I'm sorry that you were scared, and that I was the cause of that. I'm sorry for keeping things from you that you should know about if we're going to be in a relationship with each other."

It feels like a herd of butterflies are trapped in Kaia's stomach, desperate to get out. Those apologies are more than she thought she'd get from Jason tonight.

He clasps his hands together, scooting a little closer to the edge of the couch. His back is rod-straight, and he looks incredibly uncomfortable. Despite the rift between the two of them, Kaia wants nothing more than to reach out and take his hand.

Acting on instinct, she closes the distance between them, and that's exactly what she does.

He's trembling a little, and it breaks her heart. Even though this is a huge step for him, and whatever he's going to tell her is definitely something that she needs to know, she decides to be kind and offer him an out.

"Jason," she begins softly, "if you're not ready..."

"I might not ever be ready," he admits. "But I know for sure that I'm not ready to lose you, so I need to tell you this."

"I didn't give you an ultimatum, you know," Kaia says.

"We're not working on a timetable here."

"I know." He nods. "I want to do this."

Kaia isn't sure that she believes him, but she's going to trust that he's telling her the truth.

"Should we get some wine?" She's teasing, but only a little. If some alcohol will help him get through this, then he should have that.

"I had a couple of shots earlier." He squeezes her hand, then brings it up to his lips, pressing a kiss on the back of it.

He takes a deep breath, then his eyes meet hers, all haunted and sad. "When I was twelve, my parents were murdered."

The admission actually takes Kaia's breath away, like a punch to the gut. She's not sure what she was expecting, but it certainly wasn't that. Kaia places her free hand on Jason's knee, and rubs the pad of her thumb back and forth. She doesn't want to breathe a word; she knows that condolences aren't what he's looking for from her anyway.

"I had an incredibly privileged childhood. My father was the CEO of a software company that he built from the ground up alongside my mother, when the two of them were straight out of college.

"My dad was more of an entrepreneur; he had a head for the creative side of things, the software development. My mom handled the business side, because Dad just didn't have time for the details. That was where she thrived.

"They were both basically married to their work, and hired help to take care of me, so I didn't miss out on the fun parts of being a kid. I had a driver who took me to and from all of my practices," he explains in what seems like one long whoosh of words, like all he wants in this world is to get them all out and be done with it.

Kaia just sits there listening, holding his hand.

"One night on my way home from soccer practice, this car cut us off at an intersection." He pauses, as he stares out into the room, his eyes glassy with unshed tears. "I can still hear the screeching of the tires as the car came to a hard stop."

Kaia can tell the story is getting more difficult for him to tell, and there's a pained look in his eyes that she can hardly bear to look at.

"Jason," she whispers, reaching up and cupping his cheek. "You don't have to-"

"Please," he says desperately, leaning into her touch. "I have to get this out."

Kaia nods. If that's what he needs, she'll make sure he gets it.

"The guy driving the car that cut us off, he got out and just…he shot my driver. He was a new guy, a replacement for a man who had just retired. I don't even remember his name, and he died just because he took a job for my family."

There's guilt wrapped around every single word that comes out of his mouth, and all Kaia can do is sit there and hold his hand, offering him whatever support she can.

"The guy opened the back door, and dragged me out, screaming. He put a cloth against my face, and I…I woke up tied to a chair in the den of my house. He..."

Jason's voice falters now, and Kaia doesn't need him to tell her exactly what happened. She's seen evidence of it all over his chest, and she's kissed every one of the scars that hasn't faded with time. Oh how she wishes she could soothe the scars she *can't* see.

"He tortured me for what seemed like *hours*."

Tears burn Kaia's eyes as she runs her thumb over Jason's knuckles. She can't imagine. Can't even fathom what it was like to live through that, and to still be living with after all these years.

"I could hear my parents screaming for me," he says, looking down at where his hand is twined with Kaia's. "They were being held in some other part of the house by another man.

"I nearly blacked out from the pain. All I can remember is the man that was holding my parents captive was yelling about money, and my dad kept telling him that he could have whatever he wanted, as long as he stopped hurting me."

"Jason," Kaia whispers, really not wanting him to go on. She can see how much this is tearing at him, opening old wounds that had closed over time. But still, he continues.

"The man who had them, he brought them down to see me just before...and I'll never forget the look in their eyes when they saw what had been done to me. Lacerations, burns...they were all over my chest and back," he says, his voice completely wrecked. He looks up at Kaia then, looking so lost and broken.

"My mother couldn't stop crying. One of the men kept telling her to shut up, but she couldn't help herself."

The tears are falling freely down his cheeks now, so Kaia reaches up and takes his face in her hands, and kisses them away. She lets her forehead rest against his for a moment, and the two of them are quiet, just existing in the same space.

Then she waits for him to continue, because she knows he will.

"Finally the police showed up," he says. "The man who took me shot my parents, and then the cops shot him and his accomplice." He swallows hard, then inhales in one quick sniff. "And I was still tied to that fucking chair, completely helpless."

Kaia isn't sure what she should do. She wants to wrap her body around his and take away the hurt, but she's not sure if an outpouring of support like that will be received as pity.

The very last thing she feels for Jason right now is pity.

Compassion, respect, and *love*, yes, those are on the list. Pity isn't anywhere on there.

Kaia moves closer, wraps her arms around Jason's middle, then pulls herself closer into his side.

"I'm so sorry that happened to you," she says. "And I'm sorry about what happened to your parents. I'm even more sorry that you had to watch it."

She runs her hand comfortingly along the column of his neck, threading her fingers through the hair at the nape, hoping the small movement brings him comfort.

"I worry about that happening to *you*," he says emphatically, his red-rimmed eyes boring into hers. "Kaia, these men went after me to get to my parents, to get them to give them money. And I'm terrified one day that will be you."

Kaia understands that completely, and she'd be lying if she said there wasn't a big part of her—a bigger part of her than she'd like to acknowledge—that wants to turn and run away. But the part of her that is falling in love with this man wants to stay right here by his side. She wants to show him that he's worth the risk, and that her feelings for him are stronger than her fear.

"Is there a reason why you think it might? Some specific, known reason?" she asks.

"You mean, have I gotten any threats specifically about you?"

When he says it like that, an involuntary shiver runs up her spine. Kaia nods. "Yes, that's what I'm asking."

"No," he replies solemnly. "I swear to god, *no*. I hired Paul and his team as a precaution when I decided I wanted to be with you. It was something that made me feel better about wanting it."

"So, hiring a security team is what made you feel okay about getting into a relationship with me and taking me out of one-night-stand territory?" she asks, curious about what his thought process was here.

"No," he says, with a fond shake of his head, his eyes still glassy with tears. "You did that. I told you; you were the first person in years who didn't react when you saw my scars. And the more time I spent with you, the more time I *wanted* to spend with you. I couldn't stay away. The thought of losing you in my life because of something that *might* happen seemed too great of a risk, but I thought that if I told you what I was worried about happening and why, that you'd run away screaming."

"Because that had happened before," she realizes, remembering the conversation she'd had with Jason a few weeks before, when he told her about the girlfriend he told the story of his scars to. "And that's why you've spent so long keeping people at arm's length."

Jason nods. "I figured that if no one knew there was someone special—if there never *was* someone special in my life—then no one could ever use that against me. Hell, I even keep the woman who took me in after my parents died at arm's length."

"This is why we stayed in all the time. This is why you kept me out of the public eye."

With pain in his eyes, he nods. "Yes. I know you were thinking that I didn't want to be seen with you. And in a way that's true, but not for the reasons you probably thought."

Kaia thinks on that, quietly letting all the pieces of the puzzle that is Jason Turner slide into place. It must've been so difficult for him, willingly pushing away his support systems because he loved them too much to let someone use them to hurt him.

The thought is actually staggering.

The desire to forgive him, to be something good in his

life, is so strong she almost gives in and does it right then and there. But if she gives in now, then he might leave her out of some important decisions in the future just to protect her, and she doesn't want a repeat of this ever again.

"I had a right to know what I was getting into regarding a relationship with you, Jason."

"I know," he says quietly, letting his head hang down in shame. "That's one of the reasons I didn't tell you, actually. Because I was worried that you wouldn't want to deal with it."

Kaia realizes that everything that happened to Jason at such a young age must've left him with a terribly low sense of self worth, given that he thinks that no one loves him enough to want to stick around. Thinking that he's not worth the risk someone would be taking to be with him. Kaia wants to disabuse him of that notion as quickly as possible.

"Say I want to deal with it," she offers. "Say you're worth that to me. What then?"

He looks up, completely surprised. "What?"

"Think we can figure out a way to make sure that I'm safe? To get ahead of any kinds of threats that might be coming our way?"

"Of course," he vows. "But-"

"And you won't make any decisions about me and my own safety without talking to me first?"

"If that's what you want," he quickly agrees, trying to tamp down the desperate hope in his voice. "Whatever you want. My only condition is that the security stays."

Given that she now knows more about what she might be facing if she stays with him, Kaia can't argue with him wanting a security team to keep an eye on her. But she does have a condition. "If the detail stays, then I want you to introduce me to them. I want to know who's doing the protecting, just in case."

Jason looks so relieved, she could kiss him.

And she's going to do just that, but she wants to make one thing clear first.

"If you ever do anything like this again, Jason…if you don't consult me about my own safety, or you just unilaterally make a decision about me without getting my input, then we're through."

"I won't do that again, I promise."

It's the answer she wanted to hear, but she's still feeling skeptical.

"You won't keep it a secret if you think telling me the truth will make me want to leave you?"

To his credit, Jason contemplates that for a moment, which gives Kaia a little bit of comfort. If he'd answered no straight away, then she'd think he was paying her lip service.

"I think yesterday made me understand that the truth will come out anyway," he explains thoughtfully. "I don't want to hide anything from you. We'll consult with the security team if anything makes you uncomfortable. *Together*. I want you in my life, and you said you didn't want to be a secret. I don't want you to be a secret, but I need to make sure we're very careful about being in the spotlight. If you'll stay with me, Kaia…" he says, bringing her hands up to his lips. "I'll do anything to keep you safe."

She believes him. More than she's ever believed anything else in her life.

In the early hours of the morning, Kaia is lying in Jason's bed with her head on his chest.

"I want to ask you something," she says, her fingers sliding across his soft skin.

"I told you, you can ask me anything." He pulls her closer, and plants a kiss on the top of her head.

"When I looked you up on the internet after we first met," she explains, feeling Jason's muscles tense beneath her hands. "How come I didn't find anything about what happened to you or your family? Surely there was news and police reports, but nothing came up at all."

A long stretch of silence follows.

"I changed my name. I'm not proud of that, but I wanted distance from everything that happened. I didn't want that to be why people recognized my name. I feel guilty about it sometimes, like I'm distancing myself from my parents, and I never wanted to do that."

Kaia turns her head, and kisses Jason's shoulder. "I don't think they'd blame you for what you did, Jason."

"I wanted to get as far away from that life as I possibly

could, and changing my name seemed to be the first step."

"What was your name? Is it okay to ask that? You don't have to tell me if you don't want to. I just thought-"

"It was Harrington," he says softly. "My last name was Harrington."

"It's a beautiful name. Why did you decide on Turner?"

"It was my mother's maiden name."

Of *course* it was. Kaia felt like she probably should've guessed that much. "I'd love to hear about them someday when you feel like sharing."

Jason's fingertips trail up and down Kaia's spine, leaving a trail of tingling heat in their wake. "I'd like that," he says. "If it's okay, could we do that another day?"

Kaia nods. "Whenever you like." She knows he's been on an emotional roller coaster over the past couple of days. It isn't pressing information for her to have; she can let this breathe, and ask him to share some other time. There are more questions she'd like to have answers to anyway, like what happened to his father's company, and why didn't Jason follow in his footsteps.

But she can wait for that. She wants to give him some time.

"Are you still up for coming with me to the fundraiser on Saturday?"

"Yes," Kaia replies. "Why?"

"There's someone coming that I'd like you to meet."

Chapter 20

Paul, Kaia, and Jason are standing in Jason's kitchen early Saturday morning, steaming hot cups of coffee in their hands.

"We're going to take you both through the back entrance, foregoing the red carpet and the photographers. I've got a few guys stationed throughout the ballroom to keep an eye out for any suspicious activity, and we're going to do our best to discourage photographs."

Jason raises an eyebrow. "Do your best?"

Without missing a beat, Paul replies, "We can't keep track of photos people take on their cell phones, Sir. Best I can do is give them a talking to if I see them trying to take one, and dissuade them from posting it online."

Even though he knows Paul can't give him one, Jason was hoping for an absolute. A guarantee.

"We won't let anything happen to her," Paul assures him. He turns and looks at Kaia. "We're going to keep you safe."

That he believes.

"I know you won't let anything happen to her," Jason replies. "If I thought you would, you wouldn't be here right now."

Paul gives him a strained smile. "Fair point."

"We have a meeting set up with my publicist first thing Monday morning," Jason informs Paul. "A follow up to the one we had yesterday about controlling the narrative here, so random pictures of Kaia and I aren't splashed all over the internet. So we can make sure we know what's out there, and can keep her safe."

"I understand, Sir."

Jason nods. "Good. I'll see you tonight."

"That dress is gorgeous on you," Jason says, as he watches Kaia carefully applying lipstick. He's leaning against the doorway that leads to his bathroom, looking at Kaia's reflection in the mirror. "Such a shame I'm going to have to throw it on the floor later."

Kaia grins, her bright red lipstick in sharp contrast against her teeth.

"This is the nicest dress I own." She pops the lid on the lipstick tube she's holding, and puts it in her small satin clutch. "It cost me almost a month's paycheck, and some respect will be paid."

"I'll pay for the cost of the dress if you just let me have my way with it. And then let me have my way with *you*."

Kaia laughs. "Oh to be rich and not care about piddly little things like taking care of the expensive clothes I own."

Jason takes a couple steps forward, drawn to the gorgeous woman before him. The back of this dress dips almost cruelly low, exposing most of Kaia's pale skin. Jason wants to run his tongue along the stretch of Kaia's spine, wants to watch the goosebumps pebble on her skin.

The flowing skirt would make it easy to hike up. He could slide his hands around the front, cup her breasts through the fabric, tweak her nipples the way he knows she likes.

He hardens at the thought, and knows that he won't be able to keep his hands off her all night during the fundraiser.

Another version of him would've counted on escaping the festivities for a quickie in a coat closet, but this is their unofficial coming out. He doesn't want someone to catch them fucking in some dark place like they're some kind of secret.

No, he's going to have her *now*.

He walks over to where Kaia's standing at the vanity, and presses his body against hers. The dress is soft and silky beneath Jason's fingers, but it's no match for the delicate smoothness of her skin.

He slides his fingertip down Kaia's spine, watching the play of her muscles as they tense. She rocks her hips back, rubbing against his rock-hard erection.

"Jason," she whispers. She plants her hands on the granite countertop, and Jason leans over her, his chest covering her back. He nibbles at the skin below her ear. "We can't," she says, disappointment coloring her tone.

"We *can*." He reaches around, and slides his hand beneath the silk panel on the front of the dress. The weight of her breast is warm in his hand, and she arches back into him when he rubs her nipple with the pad of his thumb. "We *will*."

She looks at his reflection in the mirror, fire in her eyes.

"Lift up your skirt."

She does as he asks, her gaze never leaving his. He reaches down, and slides his fingers through the warm wetness at the center of her thighs.

"Fuck," he growls. "You're not wearing any panties."

Kaia gives him a sly grin. "Surprise."

He presses his thumb against her clit, rubbing it in a slow, maddening circle.

"You're so wet," he observes.

"I was from the moment I saw you looking at me the way you were."

"How was I looking at you?"

She arches her back, giving Jason access to her neck. He takes full advantage of it, nipping at her earlobe, then sucking at the sensitive skin where he can feel her pulse point beneath his lips.

"You were looking at me like you wanted to *devour* me."

He does. He wants to devour her. He wants to *possess* her,

and he can't wait any longer.

"Spread your legs."

She does as he asks, and he undoes his pants, tugging them down until his erection springs free.

Jason wraps his arm around Kaia's waist, lines himself up with her wet heat, and slides inside.

Kaia lets out a soft cry as he fills her that makes him rock his hips, hoping he can get her to let out another sound just like that one. They're both watching each other in the mirror as Jason rocks in and out of her.

His fingertips glide against her clit as he does his damnedest to help her find her pleasure. She's so close, almost there…her face is twisted in pleasure, and Jason can't look away from her.

He needs more, *more*…

He picks up the pace, their hips slamming together as he tries to get deeper still. He's on the verge of coming, but he can't let himself fall until she does, so he doubles his attention on her clit, rubbing faster. Harder.

Kaia moans out his name, her eyes screwed shut.

He leans forward until his raspy stubble rubs against her neck. "Come for me, Kaia. Come on."

A few more thrusts, and she's contracting around him, pulling him with her into blissful oblivion.

As they both come down, smiling dopily at each other in the mirror, all sated and relaxed, Jason knows this is going to be an incredible night.

At the fundraiser, Jason walks through the crowd, confidently mingling with his friends with Kaia on his arm. She's personable, and funny, and everyone pretty much loves her, just as he knew they would.

If a few of his friends seem shocked that he seems to have settled down a bit, Jason does his best to ignore them. He's disappointed that Chase had to cancel at the last minute in order to make an emergency trip to China to deal with some supply chain issues with his company. There will be time for them to meet later. Lots of time, Jason hopes.

Still, he was one of two people at this party Jason was looking most forward to introducing Kaia to.

The second person is walking toward them wearing an elegant gown, and a beatific smile on her face.

"Jason," Elise says fondly, standing on her tiptoes in order to reach him for a hug. "How are you?"

"I'm well," he replies.

"I can see that." She smiles at Kaia. "I'm guessing it has a lot to do with this beautiful young lady right here."

Jason slides his hand down to rest on the small of Kaia's back in a show of support. "It does," he replies, beaming down at her.

"Kaia, this is Elise Whittington. She was my mother's best friend. She took me in and raised me after my parents died. Elise, this is my girlfriend, Kaia."

Elise's entire face softens at the mention of the world 'girlfriend,' and she looks up at Jason with the kind of affection and pride he hasn't seen from her in a long time.

"Kaia," Elise says softly. "It's so nice to meet you."

"It's nice to meet you, too."

"You're just as lovely as Jason described you."

With a blush, Kaia looks down at the ground, then gives Jason a quick glance. "Thank you," she replies.

"I never thought I'd see the day," Elise teases, slapping Jason lightly on the arm. "Tell me, Kaia, what is it that you do?"

"I own a small graphic design business," she explains. "I work on corporate logos, things like that. Jason told me you're a professor at Stanford."

"That's right! Macroeconomics. But I'm not going to elaborate on that, unless you're looking for a good cure for insomnia," Elise replies with a laugh. "Are you having a good time?"

Kaia nods enthusiastically. "I am. I've never been to something like this before."

Elise steps forward, and slides her hand through the crook of Kaia's elbow, then leads her toward the door. "They're all the same," she says. "Write a check, eat terrible food, then get bored to death by the lack of conversation."

Kaia lets out an unguarded laugh. "That's kind of what I figured."

"We've all made our donations," she says. "There's a darling cafe just around the block that's a bit of a secret. Why don't we all go get some coffee there? I'd love to get to know the woman who makes Jason smile like he's looking at the sun."

Kaia grins, and looks back at him, like she wants him to give her the okay. He's more than happy to do that; when he decided to introduce Kaia to Elise, the two of them getting along like this was just about all he could've hoped for.

When they exit the building, Jason looks around, and notices that Paul isn't far behind them. Elise is chattering away, and Kaia's laughing at something she said. Jason's lost in the sound of it, and that's when a loud shot rings out through the crowd.

He acts on instinct, wrapping his arms around Kaia and Elise, shielding their bodies from view of the street, pressing their backs against the nearest building.

He's got them covered from almost every angle. Whoever's shooting at them will have to get through him first.

Jason is wild-eyed and frantic, his heart pounding out of his chest, breathing ragged. If he can just keep them protected long enough for Paul to find whoever's shooting at them, everything will be okay...

"Jason."

"*Jason*."

He's pulled out of his thoughts by Kaia's gentle but insistent voice, and her hand cupping his cheek.

"What? What is it?"

"It was just a car backfiring," she explains slowly, like he's some kind of wild animal she doesn't want to scare off. "It's okay. We're okay."

"It was just a car?" he asks, a little dazed and confused.

She smiles sadly. "Yeah, just a car. We're fine."

His gaze shifts to Elise, wanting to make sure she's okay. She gives him a soft, sad smile, and he never wants to see that look of pity in her eyes again.

Later that night, Jason sits alone in his office in the loft of his apartment. Kaia's asleep downstairs in his bed, and Elise took the guest room for the night. After witnessing the wild look in his eyes after the car backfired this evening, she insisted on staying here with him instead of at her hotel.

Truthfully, Jason doesn't mind. Even though there wasn't any real danger tonight, he'd much rather have the two of them here, under his roof, where he knows they're safe.

He's about halfway through his second glass of scotch, when he hears a soft knock on the door. Jason looks up and sees Elise standing there, in the same cotton bathrobe she's worn since he was younger.

"You don't have to worry about me," he explains, hoisting his glass in the air. "I'm fine."

"You're not fine." Elise walks into the office, and sits down in the chair opposite Jason. "I think tonight proves that."

"I've talked to someone about it," he says, hoping to forego the therapy talk. Again. "I'm as fine as I'm ever going to be."

"I love you, you know. I'd do anything for you. And all I've ever wanted was for you to be happy, despite everything that happened when you were younger."

"I think I've done a damned fine job of that," Jason says, putting his glass down on the desk.

"You have. A *fine* job. But seeing you tonight, the way you reacted, Jason…"

"Please don't start." He's not in the mood to go another round with Elise about Post Traumatic Stress Disorder. Especially not tonight.

"I have to start, Jason. I *have* to. Because you're haunted by this idea that who you are has put a target on your back."

"It put a target on Mom and Dad," he says bitterly.

Elise reaches out and places one of her hands on his, her eyes full of unshed tears and sadness. "No," she says quietly. "It didn't."

Jason isn't sure if the liquor is making Elise's words difficult to process, or if she just isn't making sense.

"What do you mean?" he asks.

"All these years, you've been thinking that what happened to your parents had everything to do with their last name and the balance in their bank accounts, and you've been living in fear that the same thing is going to happen to you. It isn't, Jason. It's not going to happen to you."

"Elise," Jason says, with worry in his voice. "What are you saying?"

She takes a deep, steadying breath, and Jason knows from

years of experience that the woman he considers his second mother is steeling herself for what comes next.

"I'm telling you that your parents aren't who you thought they were." A tear slips down her cheek. "And I want to tell you what actually happened that night."

Chapter 21

Kaia wakes to the sound of muffled voices, roused from a light, gentle sleep. Disoriented, she rolls over, reaching for Jason, who isn't there. Her hand slides across cool sheets, which tells her he's been gone a while.

A quick panic rushes through her, and she sits upright, the sheets falling across her waist. Her heart pounds against her ribcage.

"Jason?" she calls. She doesn't get a response. Instead, she hears more muffled voices. Jason's, along with someone who sounds a lot like Elise.

She looks over at the clock on Jason's bedside table.

It's 3:27. Kaia had fallen asleep in his arms not even two hours ago, after she'd done her damnedest to distract him from the events earlier in the evening. She'd been haunted by the look in his eyes as he pressed her against the wall of the building, blocking his body with hers.

He'd been so shaken afterwards, that all she wanted to do was feel his skin on hers, and make him feel so good that he forgot the panicked helplessness she'd seen written all over his face.

He came three times before he finally fell asleep, exhausted.

Looks like it hadn't lasted very long.

Jason's raised voice reverberates throughout the apartment, and Kaia slides out of bed, slipping one of Jason's old t-shirts over her head on the way out.

Muted light filters out of Jason's office into the hallway, and Kaia follows the rumbling of voices. She doesn't want to eavesdrop, but she also wants to be there for Jason if he needs her.

Elise's loud, pleading voice is what makes her run to the door, desperate to see what's going on.

Jason is standing on one side of his desk, his fingers threaded through his hair, his red-rimmed eyes looking at Elise in disbelief. She can *feel* his tension from all the way across the room. It's written all over his body.

Elise sits in the chair across from the desk, looking completely defeated. Tears are streaming down her face, and her arms are outstretched, palms up, like she's pleading. There's desperation in her eyes, like her whole world hinges on whatever Jason does next.

"Jason?" Kaia says quietly, taking a tentative step forward. "Is everything okay?"

It takes him a few seconds to fully register Kaia's presence, then his gaze flits to hers, and he looks like a drowning man. Completely, utterly lost.

Kaia slowly walks over to him, not wanting to do anything that will make him push her away, or retreat back into himself like she knows he's accustomed to doing. The newfound openness with each other that they've shared since Jason shared his past with her is still so fragile.

Kaia doesn't want to do anything to break it.

When she finally makes her way over to him, Kaia reaches out and slides her hand across Jason's back. He relaxes against her touch; the tension that was there just seconds earlier melts away. Some is still there, but he's more relaxed than he had been, and Kaia considers that a win.

"It's okay," she says softly, as her hand glides across his back.

When he looks down at her, still lost, he says, "It's not okay."

Kaia decides not to talk him out of it before she knows what's actually going on. He and Elise have been arguing, that much is obvious. The tension in the air is thick, and she could hear them before she walked in here. Apart from how wrecked Jason looks, Elise seems ready to get down on her knees and plead with him at any moment.

"What's going on?" Kaia asks.

"Elise was just leaving."

Elise lets out a quiet sob, says, "Jason, *please*."

Kaia is completely confused. The whole reason Elise is staying at the apartment tonight is because she wanted to keep an eye on Jason after what happened earlier. And Jason had told Kaia that he felt better having Elise near.

Clearly, a lot has happened since she's been asleep.

Jason brings his hand up and pinches the bridge of his nose. "Just go, please, Elise. I can't do this tonight. My driver's waiting for you downstairs. He'll take you wherever you want to go."

Jason has no family left; Elise is the closest thing he has. Kaia can't wrap her mind around what could've happened to make the situation change so suddenly, and she doesn't want to let Elise go without giving Jason the chance to cool off. She doesn't want him to regret anything he says or does here, and if she can possibly keep that from happening, she's going to.

"I'm worried about you," she tells him. "Let's just go back up to bed, and sleep on it, okay? Don't do anything you're going to regret."

Jason puts his arm around Kaia, and pulls her close, pressing a kiss to the top of her head.

"I just need some time." He looks to Elise, who's clearly gutted, and repeats the same thing. "I need some time."

Elise gives the two of them a sad smile, and watches the way Jason's hand slides across Kaia's shoulder. "Okay. I can give that to you."

"The driver-"

"Isn't necessary," Elise finishes. "I think we both know that now."

"I don't want you going out alone," Jason says. "It's late, and I'll feel better knowing you got back to your hotel okay."

Elise takes a deep breath, and nods. She stands, and gives Kaia a watery grin. "It was very nice to meet you, Kaia. I hope we'll get the chance to get to know each other better in the future."

Kaia nods. "I'd like that very much. I enjoyed meeting you, too."

She pauses, like she thinks Jason might change his mind. When he doesn't, she turns and walks out, shutting the door behind her.

Jason sighs heavily, and sits down on the edge of his desk. His shoulders are slumped, his head bowed. Kaia wants nothing more than to be there for him, to be someone he can lean on and talk to, but she doesn't want to press him.

She'd really like it if he'd open up on his own.

She steps between his legs, and he grips her hips, moving her forward, close enough so he can rest his forehead against her chest. Kaia reaches up and slides her fingers through his hair, gently scratching his scalp the way she knows he likes.

"Are you okay?"

Jason lets out an unsteady breath. "No."

Admitting it right away is something new. "Wanna talk about it?" Kaia almost immediately second-guesses herself, following that up with a quick, "It's okay if you're not ready, I-"

"She lied to me."

Kaia expected him to say a lot of things, but that definitely isn't one of them.

"About what?"

He swallows, running his hands up and down her sides, and the slide of the cotton against her skin is the only sound in the room for a long time.

"She lied to me about my parents. About why they were... about why they were killed."

Kaia's hands still in Jason's hair as she absorbs what he just told her. He's built his whole life around his parents' death, around preventing something like that from happening ever again. He refused to let himself have relationships because of it. Hell, even once he opened up to her, his past had been one of the reasons he nearly lost her.

To learn that all of that was based on a lie...

"Why were they targeted?" Kaia asks.

Jason lets out a short, bitter laugh. "Turns out they weren't the kind of people I thought they were."

The way his voice breaks when he says it, the heartsickness in it, makes Kaia pull Jason a little closer. She remembers the look on his face when he told her about his mother and father, the sheer admiration in his eyes. The pain that they were both taken from him much too soon. She's so glad she's here with him. She's happy he's letting her in.

Kaia rubs Jason's shoulders, then presses a kiss against the top of his head. He raises his head from where it was cradled against her chest, and she wants to do whatever she can to make sure she never sees this look on his face again.

"All these years I thought they were murdered because we were rich, because there were people out there who wanted what we had and were willing to do whatever they had to in order to take it."

His voice wavers, and Kaia's heart breaks. His eyes are watery, and even though she doesn't know exactly what he's getting ready to tell her, she thinks he's doing a remarkable job of holding himself together.

"Why…" Kaia can't bring herself to ask him outright why they were murdered, so she settles for an easier question. "What kind of people were they?"

Jason takes a deep breath, then answers, "Thieves."

He must read the shock written on her face, because he doesn't wait for her to respond to that, he just continues. "They built an empire on software that they stole from someone else."

Kaia doesn't need Jason to tell her that the 'someone else' he's speaking about is one or both of the men who were in his house that night.

"The guy who killed them, it was his software. My dad hired him as a contractor, then stole the code. He made it better, my mom marketed it, and the two of them made unspeakable amounts of money off of it. This," he says, motioning to the scars on his chest, "was part of the payment. My parents' lives were part of the payment."

Kaia leans forward, and wraps him up tight. Even though he's so much larger than she is, he feels so small in this moment, in her arms.

And she hears what he doesn't say. That him living his life in fear that everyone he loved was going to be taken from him was also part of the payment.

Kaia doesn't know what to say to him. She doesn't know what he needs or wants to hear. She feels completely helpless, and all she knows how to do is hold him, to kiss him, and to be here for him in whatever way he needs her to be.

"Did the mens' families not have any claim on the estate, or…" Perhaps it's not the right time to ask such a question, but Kaia can't help herself.

"From what Elise says, they were both estranged from their families," Jason explains. "So there was no claim on the estate. I'm not sure I believe her."

Kaia decides to be the voice of reason. "Why would she lie at this point?"

Jason shrugs halfheartedly. "I never thought she'd lie in the first place, so…honestly, I don't know."

"She wanted you to have good memories of your parents, Jason. What they did professionally has nothing to do with how much they loved you. She wanted you to have that, even though you couldn't have them."

He looks up at her, utterly wrecked. Like he hadn't completely understood her reasoning until now. He seems calmer, if not less upset.

"It makes sense, Jason," Kaia whispers, sliding a soothing hand up and down his arm. "How long did she know?"

"She said she found out shortly before my parents were killed. She was stunned, too. I remember that Elise hadn't come around much right before their deaths, but I never knew why."

Knowing how betrayed she felt probably compelled Elise to want to keep it from Jason. Having her own memories of her friend ruined would've made her do whatever she had to in order to keep Jason's intact.

Kaia knows this isn't the time to bring that up, though.

"Why on earth did she decide to tell you this tonight?"

Jason wraps his fingers around Kaia's, then brings the back of her hand up to his lips.

"I'm sure it comes as no surprise to you that I've been a little closed off from her."

From everyone, Kaia wants to tease, but she doesn't. She understands now. "You told me you were afraid of losing her the same way you lost your parents."

Jason's quick intake of breath and the forlorn look in his eyes makes Kaia realize that this probably wasn't the best time to bring that up. Still, he moves past it.

"Yeah. She knows that's why. She understands that about me. And it's been a long, long time since she's seen me happy. You. You make me happy."

Even though it's an inopportune moment, Kaia feels happiness roll through her when she hears those words. A small smile quirks her lips. She likes that she makes him happy. She wants to be the person who does that always.

"Tonight she told me that she never thought she'd see me look that happy again. She wanted me to hold onto that. And after the car backfired, then she saw what happened...I think she thought maybe those fears would come back. That they'd take hold, and make me push you away. She didn't want me to throw this away just because I was scared. I think seeing it in action freaked her out."

Kaia understands that. "And she wanted you to know that there wasn't anything to be scared of."

He nods. "For a minute I thought maybe she was lying. I wanted her to be lying, because I thought I'd rather live in a world where there was a threat I could actively try to prevent than a world where my parents were liars and thieves. But...I know she wouldn't do that to me. She's telling me the truth."

"Now which world would you rather live in?"

He squeezes her fingers. "I...I don't know." He pulls away from her, and walks a couple of steps away, his hands fidgeting at his sides. "I'm angry, I'm relieved. I'm...a lot of things."

"It's okay to be all those things," Kaia assures him. "You have time to sort all of this out."

He looks up at her with tired eyes and a soft smile, before closing the distance between them in two long strides.

He kisses her, short and sweet, then rests his forehead against hers. "I'm glad you're here."

She smiles. "I'm glad I'm here, too." And even though she knows he's not going to get much rest for what little is left of tonight, she holds out her hand and suggests it anyway. "Why don't you come to bed and see if you can get some rest?"

He takes her hand, and lets her lead him back to his bedroom.

Chapter 22

Dawn is breaking across the horizon, streaming in through the windows in Jason's apartment. He's sitting at the bar in his kitchen, and his eyes are sandy and heavy from exhaustion. He was awake all night, staring up at the ceiling while Kaia used him as a pillow, unable to turn off his brain and just *sleep*.

All he could think about was Elise's face as she told him the truth. The hitched, sobbing breaths as she told him the truth about his mother and father, the two people he'd always looked up to, both in life and in death.

And all of it was a lie.

It felt like a slap in the face.

Even though he told Kaia that he knew Elise wouldn't tell him this if it wasn't the actual truth, he still let those thoughts invade his mind last night as he listened to Kaia's soft breathing, hoping her peace would quiet them down.

Elise told him that she'd been thinking about telling him the truth for years. That she was afraid his fear of letting people close was going to lead to a long, lonely life for him.

That fear of hers was always fighting her desire to keep his parents' positive memory alive for him.

In the calmer moments that he's had over the past few hours, he can't really be mad at her for keeping up the charade for all these years. Especially when his childhood was ripped from him when he was all of twelve years old.

Jason doesn't even know who he's angry with. His parents. Elise. *Everyone.* It's a heavy weight of emotion that's settled in the pit of his stomach, and it gives him a new target every few minutes.

There's another part of him that's absolutely relieved to know the truth, and he hates it. He hates that the bright side of all this is knowing that he doesn't have to be worried anymore, that he doesn't have to look over his shoulder wondering who's following him, who's waiting to take everything he loves away.

It's a relief he didn't know he was so desperate for until he had it.

On the countertop in front of him is a box of old photos that he had tucked away in his closet. For so long it's been too painful to open it up, and shuffle through the memories. It's painful now, too, in a way that it hasn't been before.

He looks at the pictures spread out before him, wondering which moments were true. Were they all really happy here?

Were all the good memories that he had actually *good*, or were those lies, too?

His father took him fishing on Saturday mornings. He carefully taught him how to bait a hook, how to cast a line. How to cook a fish over the camp fire.

Jason's mother always told him to follow his passion in life, not to do something because he thought he should, but to do it because he wanted to. That's how he ended up working in investments, instead of following in his parents' footsteps, taking up the family business.

Jason wonders now if his mother's advice was completely on the up-and-up. He wonders if she gave it to him because that's what she truly believed and wanted for him, or if she told him that to steer him away from the family business.

To keep their secrets hidden.

How long did they expect to keep it up? Did they think the past would never come knocking?

Elise told him last night that his parents gave the original creators of that software a small stipend. Were they dumb enough to think that they would always settle for pennies when there were millions to be had?

Jason pulls another photo out of the box, and feels an unsettled knot in his chest. These are all questions that he's never going to have the answer to, and he's going to have to accept that.

Just the thought of going through the rest of his life never knowing is unnerving.

"Good morning," Kaia says, as she sleepily strolls into the kitchen.

She looks as tired as he feels. He doubts she got much rest, but she did at least manage to fall asleep, and he's glad for that. Her weight on his chest, and the feel of her breathing kept him anchored. It kept him calm despite the chaos in his mind.

"Morning," he replies.

She shuffles over to him, and wraps her arms around his neck. Jason never bothered to get dressed, so he's sitting there in a pair of sweatpants. Kaia's still in one of his old shirts. He loves the sight of her in it, the way she looks so at home here while she's wearing it. He loves the feeling of the old, worn cotton as it slides against his skin when she hugs him from behind.

He turns in his chair, and wraps her up in his arms, burying his face in her hair. He wants this all day, wants to lounge around just the two of them. It's been so long since he's let himself have a Sunday of doing nothing, and he knows he won't be able to work. He can't focus on anything too taxing today.

He just wants Kaia to stay right here in his arms, and help him make sense of the new world as he knows it.

She gives him a quick kiss, then leans over and steals a quick sip from his coffee mug, her nose wrinkling at the bitterness.

He likes it black, she likes a little cream and sugar.

He loves that he knows that about her now.

"Whatcha looking at?"

"Some pictures," he replies, even though that much is obvious. Kaia sidles up to him, and he wraps his arm around her waist, letting his hand rest on her hip. It's moments like these that make him wonder how he managed to live so long without *this*.

Just a touch of her hand makes the weight of the world on his shoulders so much easier to bear, since he has someone to share it with. She helps lighten the load.

Jason pulls Kaia up onto his lap, and wraps an arm around her middle to keep her where she is. He uses his free hand to slide the group of pictures across the counter, where Kaia will be able to see them better.

"Is this you?" she asks, taking a photo by its edges.

Jason laughs. She's going to see all the good, all the bad, and all the ugly this morning.

"Yes," he replies. "It wasn't my best look." Cowlick. Braces. *Definitely* not his best look.

"I think we all go through ugly phases. I think the whole point of them is so that nasty teenagers can pick out our biggest weaknesses and make us insecure about them for the rest of our lives." Kaia sighs, and brings the picture closer. "At least, that's what happened to me."

Jason smiles, and presses a kiss against Kaia's neck. "I can't imagine you going through an ugly phase."

She playfully slaps his arm. "Flatterer. I'll show you my middle school yearbook. Sixth through eighth grade were a nightmare. I looked like a frizzy-haired rail."

He doesn't believe her. "I bet you were beautiful then, like you're beautiful now."

His voice is soft and earnest, and it makes Kaia give him this gentle smile that lights up her whole face. She turns and kisses him, before focusing on the pictures again.

"You and your dad really liked to fish, huh?"

She picks up a photo of him and his father. Jason's giving the camera a goofy grin. That was the summer that his two front teeth fell out, right before he and his father caught the biggest bass Jason had ever seen.

His father is holding it in the picture; it's taller than Jason.

"It was our thing," he replies. "He'd wake me up early on Saturdays, at the crack of dawn, and we'd drive down to his favorite lake. From sunrise to about ten, it was just the two of us. Our time. It made me feel…"

Emotions clog his throat, making it impossible to get the words out. He doesn't even know what he'd say if he could, and maybe that's for the best.

"He made you feel special," Kaia says.

And yes, that's exactly it. He leans forward, and rests his chin on her shoulder. "Yeah," he breathes.

"No matter what your parents did professionally," she says, sliding her hand across his forearm where it's wrapped around her middle, until her fingers twine with his, "that doesn't change the fact that you're their son, and they loved you."

Despite all the doubts that are niggling at the back of his

mind, he believes her. And with that, he's had about his fill of wallowing for today.

"Have any plans today?" Jason asks.

"Depends."

"On what?"

"On what you're doing. I kind of wanted to hang out with my guy," she replies. He likes the sound of those words on her lips. "I think he needs me."

Jason grins. "He does." He needs her more than she'll probably ever know. He brushes her hair to the side, so he can suck on her neck.

She melts into him as his hand slides up beneath her shirt, and he cups her breast.

"Make me forget," he whispers. "Make me forget about the world for a little while."

Kaia slides off his lap, and leads him over to the couch, where he sits down in front of her. Her long hair is all messy and sexy, and the v-neck of his t-shirt is hanging off of her shoulder.

He wants nothing more in this moment more than he wants her. In any and every way.

She drops down to her knees, then leans forward and scrapes her nails down his chest, over battered, scarred flesh that she treats like it was smooth as silk.

He relaxes into the cushions, watching the way Kaia's fingers trip along the waistband of his pants. She tugs them down until his erection springs free, and she gives him a lascivious smile as she takes his cock in her hand.

She opens her mouth, flicks her tongue across his tip, then rubs it along the sensitive underside.

Jason sucks in a sharp breath through clenched teeth, and slides his fingers through her hair as she takes him in her mouth.

He's seen it countless times at this point, but he doesn't think he'll ever see anything sexier than Kaia's lips wrapped around him.

He wants to tell her that. He wants to tell her so many things.

Instead, he lets himself get lost in the warm pleasure of her mouth, and tries not to think for a while.

"You're taking this a lot better than I thought you would," Chase says, as he cuts a piece of steak and pops it into his mouth. "I'm still fucking floored."

Jason grins, and settles back into the booth, before taking a sip of his beer. It's been too long since the two of them have had a casual lunch together. He's going to have to make an effort to make this a regular thing.

"I've had a few days to let it sink in."

"I can't believe it," he says, shaking his head. "All this time."

Jason nods. "All this time."

"Elise must've been pretty gutted to tell you all that," Chase says. He's spent a fair bit of time with Elise throughout the years, and knows that she thinks of Jason as her own son.

"She was," he replies, feeling regret settle in his bones. "I haven't spoken to her since."

Chase furrows his brow, and Jason knows what he's going to say. He's going to reprimand him for shutting her out.

"I just asked her for a little time," he says quickly, wanting to spare Chase the lecture. "I was completely blindsided by it, and after the night I'd had, tensions were running high. It was better that way."

Chase nods. "I've seen you angry, and I tend to agree. Better to get some space than say something you'd regret. Figure out what you're gonna do about it yet?"

With a halfhearted shrug, Jason says, "Not yet." It's not like he's planning to give her the silent treatment forever. He just needs some time to *think*.

"Anything she kept hidden, man, you know she did it because she thought it was what was best for you, right?"

Deep down, Jason knows that.

"And I'm not trying to guilt trip you," Chase continues, "but my mom told me she's pretty torn up."

That surprises him. "Your mom knows?"

"No, no." Chase puts his beer down and waves his hand. "She asked me if you'd talked to Elise lately, because she's been kind of down lately. Not herself. She won't tell my mom what's wrong, though."

That hits Jason harder than he anticipated. He loves Elise,

he doesn't want her hurting. Especially not when she only did what she thought was best for him, both in hiding the truth, and then in revealing it.

"I won't let it fester," Jason assures his friend. "I'll get in touch with her."

Chase grins. "Good. Seems like progress for you. Not too long ago, it probably would've taken years for you to come around."

Jason grins and nods, taking his friend's gentle teasing in stride.

"Things are…it's easier with Kaia. Now that everything's out in the open, she…she helps me in ways I never thought someone could."

"I never thought I'd see the day," Chase replies, gently shaking his head as he raises his beer to his lips. "You, settling down, and not even seeming the least bit freaked out by it."

"I'm not freaked out at all. It's actually nice."

Chase dramatically clutches his chest. "Who are you, and what have you done with my best friend?"

"You better be careful," Jason says, picking up his bottle, and pointing the neck in Chase's direction. "If I fall into domestic bliss, I might just start trying to set you up."

"Double dating." Chase shivers, and makes a little retching noise.

"One day, it'll hit you before you even know it."

"Not a chance. I'm glad you're happy, though. You deserve

it, after everything."

"I am happy. And I want you to meet her."

Chase nods. "Name the time, name the date. I'm there."

Chapter 23

The time is 7PM. The date is that Sunday.

And Kaia's so nervous that she wants to crawl out of her skin. Jason has two people in his life that he's incredibly close to. She's already met Elise, and liked her, and is well on her way to helping Jason mend his relationship with her.

Chase is the second. His oldest, dearest friend. She wants to make a good impression. She desperately wants Chase to like her.

She's pretty sure Elise does, so she's at least doing well in that department.

It doesn't do anything to calm her nerves as far as Chase is concerned, and she's not even really *doing anything* for this get together. Jason ordered dinner, it's on its way. The red is uncorked and on the counter breathing.

The table is set, waiting for the food to be delivered.

All Kaia has to do is wait.

She chooses to do her waiting in front of the mirror that hangs on the back of Jason's bedroom door, checking that her hair is in place, that her dress isn't wrinkled.

It's not like she's trying to look good for Chase, she's just trying to look good, *period*. Both his and Jason's romantic histories have been splashed across the pages of the city tabloids. She's not trying to compare to those other women, exactly, it's just that she knows there have been a lot of others, and she wants to rate somewhere.

It's ridiculous, she knows this. She has Jason's heart and commitment, and that's the most important part. There's just a not-so-small part of her that wants his friend to agree with his choices.

Some wine would probably help stop this train of thought right in its station.

"Relax," Jason says, walking up behind her. His presence startles her. It doesn't take long until she's calmed by the look in his eyes.

Appreciative. Wanting.

He's dressed casually, in a Henley and a nice-fitting pair of jeans. She's wearing her favorite sheath dress. Not too fancy, but she looks like she gives a damn about her appearance, which is what she's going for.

It's black, and hugs all the right curves. Jason loves it on her, which was one of the reasons she chose it, if she's being honest.

"You look beautiful," he says, clasping her wrist as she goes to smooth over her skirt for the thousandth time. "Amazing." He leans down and presses a kiss against her bare shoulder. "Gorgeous."

"If you're not careful, your friend is going to walk in on something pretty indecent."

He laughs, a hot breath that glides across her skin. "He's not going to just walk in. The door's locked."

Kaia arches against Jason's chest as he sucks on the curve of her neck. His hand slides up to her breast, and right on cue, the doorbell rings.

Kaia pulls away from Jason with a laugh, and he just lets out a long-suffering groan.

"What's the opposite of being saved by the bell?"

With an angry little grumble, Jason replies, "Cockblocked by the bell?"

"If tonight goes well, I just might make it up to you."

Jason's eyes light up. "Promise?"

Kaia shakes her head, takes his hand, and leads him to the front door. "C'mon."

"I'm so glad I'm finally getting the chance to meet you," Chase says with a genuine smile.

He's sitting across from her at Jason's table, empty takeout containers and empty plates all around them.

They've gotten into the wine, and all the nervousness Kaia felt earlier has melted away. It's a little bit because of the alcohol, and a little bit because Chase is even more charming and friendly than Kaia could've imagined.

Things are going *so* well, and she doesn't feel at all like a third wheel, which is something she really worried about.

"It's good to finally meet you, too."

"I told Jason that I've never seen him this happy. I was almost convinced that you weren't real. This is one instance where I'm happy to be proven wrong."

"I'm very real," she replies, sliding her hand down to cover her stomach. "And very stuffed. That was delicious."

"It was," Jason agrees.

"Knowing the owners helps," Chase explains, leaning back in his chair. "One call, and they'll make anything for you. Just tell them you want a special meal for dinner with a special woman."

There isn't an ounce of flirtation in the way he says those words, but Kaia feels a smile creeping across her lips just the same. She can't help but laugh, and shake her head.

"What?" Chase asks.

"You're very charming."

Jason laughs. "He's laying it on a little thick this evening."

Kaia turns her head so she can get a good look at Jason, where he's sitting beside her. She narrows her eyes. "You don't think I'm a special woman?"

He leans in and gives her a quick peck. "You're the most

special woman I know," he replies quickly. "But I'm the only one in this room who's allowed to think that."

Kaia doesn't mind Jason's possessive streak, really. In fact, she thinks she quite likes it when it comes out amongst friends. Especially when it makes him slide his arm along the back of her chair, and gently trail his fingertips up and down her bare arm like he's doing right now.

Yeah, she likes that *a lot*.

She smiles despite herself, and looks between the two old friends. "You two together are quite a force to be reckoned with."

"It's a good thing we went to college across the country from each other," Chase says with a laugh. "The world might never have recovered. In prep school, though? That's a different story."

"We were partners in crime," Jason replies.

"Yep." Chase nods, then takes a sip of his wine. "We got into a ton of trouble."

"And charmed our way out of it."

"*Almost* all of it," Chase amends.

Kaia figured as much. Chase and Jason are so naturally charismatic individually, and she's only just starting to get a taste of what a force that is when they're together. She can only imagine how concentrated the powers are when they're together and actually *trying*.

"What kind of trouble did you two get into?"

Chase laughs. "Oh, you know. Typical asshole teenager

stuff. Breaking into the headmaster's office and bringing his furniture out onto the school's front lawn, ditching school to steal my father's boat and take it for a spin on the bay."

Kaia laughs so loud and so suddenly that she actually has to cover her mouth.

"What?" Jason and Chase say simultaneously, both looking pretty confused. It's cute, Kaia thinks.

"That is *not* typical teenager stuff," she replies. "That's spoiled rich kid stuff."

They both pretend to be offended.

Jason's hand slides down her back. "Oh? Why don't you tell us what typical teenager stuff is, then."

"I thought you would've TP-ed some houses or something. But where you guys grew up, the TP budget probably would've been massive."

That gets Jason interested. "What would you know about TP-ing houses?" he teases.

Kaia innocently shrugs. "Not much. I never did it myself," she continues, even though Chase and Jason are giving her their best disbelieving looks. "But my sister dated this guy in high school who was a master at it. He was like a TP ninja; so stealthy."

Kaia looks over at Jason, and she swears he almost looks a little jealous that she's complimenting another guy's TP-ing skills.

Men.

"If you weren't doing that, then what was your poison for a

little mischief making in high school?" Chase asks her.

"I grew up in Iowa. There was only so much mischief to be made. We did pretty low-level stuff, what *I* would consider to be typical teenaged troublemaking."

"Like?"

"Like getting drunk under the bleachers. Making out under the bleachers. Doing other stuff under the bleachers," she says with a laugh.

Chase leans forward, resting his elbows on the table, completely interested in the turn this conversation has taken. Jason's hand stills on her back. She turns and gives him a soft smile, then rests her hand on his thigh, not wanting him to get too uptight over things that happened years ago.

"Sounds like those bleachers saw a ton of action." Chase says.

"So did the people under them."

Chase lets out a loud laugh. "I like you," he says to Kaia. Then, he turns to Jason. "You hang onto this one."

Jason gives Kaia a soft, smitten smile. "I'm planning on it."

A swarm of butterflies slams right into her ribcage, knocking the breath right out of her. She's never wanted to be held onto so badly in her entire life.

"Being from Iowa, did you ever go cow tipping?" Chase asks.

Kaia shakes her head. "No way. Not all of Iowa is desolate farmland, and that's a total bumpkin stereotype! How would you like it if I did that to you?"

"Stereotype?"

Kaia nods. "Yeah, like, assumed that you two…I don't know, stole a Lamborghini or something."

Jason barks out a laugh. "No, no Lamborghinis."

"We did take Kyle's dad's Maserati out once though, remember that?"

With a soft laugh, Jason's hand resumes its comforting circuit, up and down her spine. Kaia leans into it.

"Guess they're stereotypes for a reason, then," Chase laughs.

"And look at you now!" Kaia raises her hands, gesturing to both Chase and Jason. "You're both fine, upstanding citizens. Who would've thought?"

"It's amazing what growing up will do for you."

Kaia looks over at Jason, and smiles. "It is. *Really* amazing."

Chapter 24

Jason sits on the edge of his bed, watching Kaia through the open bathroom door. She's standing in front of what he's quickly starting to think of as *her* sink, brushing her teeth. She's wearing nothing but a bra and a flimsy pair of underwear. Her hair is down, and she looks as gorgeous as he's ever seen her.

He likes knowing that after she puts the toothbrush down, she's going to tie her hair back, and rub a cloth across her face that removes all of her makeup. After that, she'll carefully pat moisturizer into her skin. Jason likes the way it smells when he nuzzles up close to her when they're trying to sleep.

This, he realizes, is *intimacy*. It's something that he's run away from for almost his whole life, and now he finds that he *craves* it.

With Kaia.

When Chase left this evening, Jason walked him out, as Kaia started clearing the table. Once his old friend was in the elevator, before the doors closed, he leaned forward and said, "Don't you dare fuck that up."

Jason wouldn't dare. He wants Kaia with him always, and he feels that down in his bones.

He knows that's a feeling he probably wouldn't have if the heaviness of the past were still weighing on him. As angry and as shocked as he was when Elise told him the truth, he finds that it quickly fizzled out. In a perfect world, he'd still be able to think about his mother and father and feel unwavering pride and respect. Knowing what they did is troubling, to say the least. It would be so easy to let that infect his memories of them, and he's entertained that more times than he cares to admit. But he believes what Kaia told him is true. Jason is their son, and despite what deception they were involved in professionally, they loved him, more than anything.

He felt loved and protected as a child, until it all fell apart. He's hung onto that pain and fear for so long, he wants to let it go.

It's time to let it go. To imagine a future free of the burdens of the past. That's what Elise gave him when she decided that the present and the promise of the future was more important than keeping his mother and father up on a pedestal.

Jason thinks it's about time he thanked her for that. She's given him more than she even realizes.

And there isn't a single part of him he's afraid to let Kaia see. He's spent so many years hiding, keeping himself covered up and closed off. It's so freeing to be able to sit here in his boxers, not worried about what Kaia will think when she sees them.

She treats his scars (both the physical, and the emotional ones) with the care they deserve, but she doesn't let them define him.

Jason never thought he'd ever want to have this, much less be lucky enough to actually find it. Now, he doesn't ever want to let it go.

He's so lost in thought—in *revelation*—he doesn't even notice Kaia standing in front of him.

He spreads his legs, and she steps right into the space he's made for her, then runs her fingers through his hair. He sighs, and closes his eyes, enjoying the way her nails lightly scratch against his scalp.

He wants to spend every night like this. With her.

"Chase loved you," he tells her, pride lacing his voice.

"Yeah?"

His eyes are still closed, but he can imagine the sweet smile on her face by her tone.

"Mmm," he agrees. "In the elevator, he told me that I better not fuck it up."

Kaia laughs. "I agree with him there."

Jason's eyelids flutter open, and he looks up at Kaia with unguarded affection written all over his face. He reaches out for her, placing his hands on her hips, where they fit perfectly, and he pulls her closer.

"I'm not going to fuck it up," he says, his voice a little broken, but full of promise.

Kaia smiles at him, then cups his face. "I know you won't."

He turns his head, and kisses her palm. "I love you, Kaia."

Her smile broadens till it's brighter than the sun. "Yeah?"

He nods. "So much."

"Then I suppose it's a good thing I love you, too."

His heart? It's *flying*. "Yeah?"

She nods. "*So* much."

Jason's hands slide up Kaia's sides, and he smiles as he watches the goosebumps bloom across her perfect skin. He leans forward, and presses a kiss right next to her belly button.

"I was kinda hoping you'd let me show you how much," he says.

"Yeah?"

He reaches up and unclasps her bra, then hooks his fingers in the waistband of her panties before slowly sliding them down her thighs.

"Mmm-hmm," he says, tilting his head up and taking one of her nipples into his mouth. He runs his tongue across the pebbled flesh, relishing in the shiver that reverberates throughout Kaia's body when he does it.

She lets out this hot, breathy moan, gripping the hair at the nape of his neck. She presses one knee into the mattress beside his hip, then the other, until she's straddling him, hot and ready against his rapidly hardening cock.

He wants her so badly, and even though he's impatient to be inside of her already, he wants to bring her to the brink, wants her to *beg* for him.

With his arm wrapped tightly around her waist, Jason flips her, so she's on her back, and he's on his knees, hovering over her. She lets out a delighted, surprised giggle, then pulls him down for a kiss.

He continues with the kisses. Down her neck, across her chest, along the length of her stomach. He nips at her hip bone, then slides his hands up the insides of her thighs, opening her legs for him.

Jason gets down on his stomach, wraps his arms around Kaia's thighs, pulling her closer to him. He leans in, and licks a stripe along her slit, making Kaia slide her fingers into his hair, gripping it tightly.

Her breathing hitches as he circles her clit, then sucks it into his mouth. She lets out a soft, breathy moan, and Jason smiles against her. He wants more of those little noises, so he reaches up and pushes two fingers inside of her, making her gasp.

"Oh god," she whines, rocking her hips as he curls his fingers up, hitting her in that place that makes her toes curl.

He doesn't have to ask her if she likes it; he knows she does. He works his fingers and his tongue in tandem, winding her up tight until she's chanting a soft, steady "please" over and over again. Jason slides his free hand up her body, tweaking her nipple as he gives her clit one last suck and flick of his tongue, and she falls apart beneath him, muscles clenching and relaxing around his fingers.

He steadily strokes her as she comes down, then kisses the inside of her thigh when she looks at him with that happy, sated look in her eyes.

"Love you," she says.

He can't help but smile at her as he crawls up her body. "I love *you*." He feels so good saying it, he doesn't ever want to stop. He knows he won't ever tire of hearing it.

"C'mere and gimme a kiss." Her words are a little slurred, and he can't help the rush of masculine pride that fills his chest. He made her look and sound like this, and he knows he's going to be doing that for the rest of her life.

He does as she asks. Their lips move together languidly, and Jason gets impossibly harder when Kaia sucks his tongue into her mouth.

She gently presses on his shoulder, and even though it isn't nearly enough pressure to actually move him, he does what she wants him to anyway. She straddles him, then works her way down his body, until she's sitting astride his legs.

Kaia leaves a trail of kisses along the band of his boxer briefs, then cups him through the fabric. She rubs his cock through the fabric, and he bucks his hips, chasing her touch.

He's so hard that it hurts. He's aching to be inside her.

Kaia slides his underwear off, tossing them somewhere on the floor. Then she sits back on his calves, and gives him a devious smile. Her hair is a little wild, falling in waves over her breasts.

She's fucking gorgeous like this.

"C'mere," he says roughly, crooking his finger towards her. All he wants is to bury himself deep inside her, to feel the weight of her on his body as she rides him.

Kaia, however, is in the mood to tease him.

She bends at the waist, letting the ends of her hair tickle his upper thighs. He can feel every breath of hers across his skin, and it sends shivers up his spine.

Whatever she wants to do to him in this moment, he's going to let her. Gladly.

She licks along the underside of his shaft, before she takes him in her mouth, all warm and wet. She works him just the way he likes, sucking and licking until he's reaching over to brush her hair out of the way so he can watch the way her lips slip up and down his sensitive, overheated flesh.

Each movement pushes him closer and closer to the brink. He's going to come soon, and he wants to be inside of her when he does.

"Kaia, *please*," he manages. "I want inside of you."

She must see the desperation in Jason's eyes, because she lifts off of him with a quick pop of her mouth, then gives him a long, slow kiss, grinding against him *right* where he wants to be.

"*Please*," he says again, not missing the fact that even though he wanted her to beg him for more, he's entirely happy that the tables have turned. "Ride me."

Blessedly, she gives in, and Jason's head lolls back as she slowly lowers herself down onto him. He lets out a long, unsteady breath. Thinks, *finally. This feels like home.*

He pushes himself up, and sits cross-legged, wrapping Kaia's legs around his waist until she's comfortable situated in his lap. He can't get as deep in this position, but the intimacy of it is what he's craving. Kaia rotates her hips, sometimes alternating the motion as he gets lost in the paradise of her body. She wraps her arms around him, their chests rubbing together as they move, his thumb rubbing quick circles on her clit, making her back arch and her breathing ragged.

Jason kisses her breasts, up the valley between them, before settling on her perfect lips.

Neither one of them is in any particular hurry to come, but eventually it becomes impossible not to chase the pleasure that's building up inside of them.

"Jason," Kaia breathes, as she presses her forehead against his. "I need…"

"What? What do you need?"

"*More,*" she begs.

She rocks against him desperately, and he picks up the pace to help her along. He's steadily losing the thread, but he's going to hang on until she comes.

"Come on," he whispers, his lips brushing the shell of her ear. Then he sucks on the sensitive part of her neck, and she's coming, holding onto him for dear life as her hips rock onto his. He fucks her through it, unable to hold on much longer, burying his face in her neck as he spills into her.

They collapse onto the bed, still tangled around each other, Kaia's head pillowed on his chest.

"Wow," she says, smiling.

"Wow," he replies, because he's too blissed out to think of any other words right now, and that one covers it just as well as any others would.

She grins, and snuggles up closer.

"Thank you," he whispers, leaning in and pressing a kiss to her forehead.

"For what?" she asks, eyebrows drawn together.

"For being here. For loving me."

Kaia balances herself on her elbow, then slides her hand up his chest until she's cupping his cheek. She leans in and gives him a soft kiss.

"There isn't anywhere else I'd rather be, or anything else I'd rather be doing."

He smiles against her mouth.

"Would you do something for me?" he asks.

Kaia nods. "Anything."

"Come to California with me. I need to go and talk to Elise."

Chapter 25

"So, you're not ever coming back, right?" Janine asks, as she fiddles with the zipper pull on Kaia's suitcase, which is lying open on top of her bed.

"What?" Kaia asks. Her voice is muffled from somewhere in her closet, where she's trying to decide whether she should bring the red dress, or the blue one. Then she realizes that she and Jason are flying to California on his *private jet*, so she can bring whatever in the hell she wants.

She takes them both off of their hangers, and tosses them over her arm before walking back into her bedroom.

"You're not coming back, are you?"

Kaia laughs. "Why wouldn't I?"

"Oh, I don't know." Janine reaches up and twirls a lock of hair between her fingers. "Cause a hot, rich guy who's totally in love with you is taking you to San Francisco on a private jet.

Why would you come home after that? He's probably got some ridiculous, to-die-for oceanfront mansion that you're going to fall in love with and never come back."

"Wow," Kaia says, carefully folding the dresses and placing them in her bag. She walks over to Janine, and makes a show of putting her hand on her forehead, like she's checking for a fever. "Are you feeling okay?"

"No!" Janine says with a laugh. "It's happening. I mean, I've been prepared for this for a while now, but…it's really happening."

Kaia is completely lost. "I have *no* idea what you're talking about."

Janine shakes her head, and gives Kaia a soft, sad smile. "Don't mind me. Just having some weird best-friend-slash-roommate separation anxiety. It'll pass."

"What's really going on?" Kaia asks, as she takes a seat next to her friend.

"I'm just sad," Janine says with a little shrug. "You're leaving."

Still completely perplexed, Kaia says, "Yes. To California. But it's just for a few days. I'll be back on Monday."

"But you won't be back here."

"I'll stay at Jason's for a while, yeah."

Janine gives her a sideways glance. "That's what I'm talking about."

"That I'll be staying at Jason's?"

Janine laughs. "No, that you'll start staying at Jason's more and more, and then you're basically just paying rent for a place to keep your stuff. It's like…it's like a really expensive closet."

"You're getting a little ahead of yourself, aren't you?"

With a little shake of her head, Janine says, "Nah. I think you're a little behind. It's already started, Kaia. And I'm happy for you, I really am. I'm just…it's totally selfish, and I get that. I'm not trying to be a jerk, I'm just a little sad for me. I feel like I'm losing you."

"You're not losing me," Kaia says emphatically.

"The last time we had a movie night was when Jason fucked up and you found out he had secret security guards tailing you."

Surely that couldn't be right. But when Kaia stopped and thought about it, she realized that Janine was right.

"Oh god. Janine, I'm-"

"It's okay," she says, finally smiling. "I don't know if you're in some kind of denial, or just really incredibly dense, but you and Jason, you're…you're it for each other."

Kaia is neither of those things. She's just been afraid to talk about everything that's going on because it's perfect right now. And she's worried that if she voices how perfect it is… something will go wrong.

Which is ridiculous, of course. But she and Jason have been through so much together in such a short amount of time, she doesn't want anything to jinx it.

But none of that excuses her for not making time for her best friend.

"When you come back, you're basically going to be living together," Janine continues. "And you're totally going to get married. Which I honestly can't wait for, because I know the bridesmaids dresses will be killer, and the meal will be amazing, no doubt. So, I'm excited about all those things, but…I just want to make sure there's room for me in all of it."

"Of course there's room for you in it," Kaia assures her, leaning over and wrapping her arms around her friend. "I promise I'm going to be better about finding a balance here." Her work is picking up; new jobs are flowing in almost faster than she can handle them, but if she's going to make this all work, she's got to learn how to maintain a healthy balance.

And that starts with making that commitment right now.

"We'll make time for girl time," Kaia suggests.

"Like a platonic date night?"

With a laugh, Kaia replies, "Yeah, something like that."

"Okay," Janine agrees. "I think that would work."

"We'll make it work."

Janine bumps Kaia's shoulder with hers. "Yeah, we will. Know what would make it easier to spend time together?"

Kaia knows she's up to something, but she plays along anyway. "What's that?"

"If you…I don't know, set me up with one of Jason's hot, eligible bachelor friends? Or even the head secret bodyguard."

"Paul?" Kaia asks, incredulous.

"Yeah! He was pretty cute."

Kaia laughs. "I'll look into it."

That placates her. "Cool. I'm going to nag you about it again, just F-Y-I."

"I would expect nothing less."

"I'm going to get serious for a minute."

That makes Kaia sit up straight, preparing herself for whatever's coming next. With Janine, she never can be too sure.

"Despite what I said earlier," she begins, taking Kaia's hand. "He makes you happy. And that makes me happy."

"I *am* happy. I never thought we'd get here, but…"

"Here you are."

Kaia nods. "Yeah."

"There's nothing I'd want more."

"Except for a…what was it? A hot, eligible bachelor friend?"

Janine laughs. "*Maybe* that."

"I'll see what I can do."

From the terrace of Elise's gorgeous condo, Kaia can see the Golden Gate Bridge. Kaia's lounging on one of the most comfortable chairs she's ever had the pleasure of sitting in, sipping one of the best wines she's ever tasted.

Elise is sitting on the chaise next to her, doing the same.

Jason is inside, taking care of some business that needed to be tended to when they landed.

A billionaire's work is never done, it seems.

"This view is gorgeous."

Elise smiles. "Isn't it? I've lived in this city my whole life, and I don't think I'll ever tire of it."

"I can't imagine you would. I've only lived in New York for a couple of years, but I feel that way about Central Park. That piece of heaven right in the city. It's one of my favorite places, and I don't think that'll ever change."

"It's nice to have your own little sanctuary."

"I think we can toast to that?"

Elise smiles, and gently taps her glass against Kaia's.

"I'm incredibly sorry that we didn't get the chance to spend more time together when we met."

Kaia shifts in her seat, feeling ever-so-slightly uncomfortable that Elise has decided to broach this subject with her. She was hoping Jason would talk to her about it and that would be that, considering that conversation is the whole reason why they're here in the first place.

"I'm sorry, too."

"I'm embarrassed of what happened that night. That you had to witness it."

Kaia gets the sense that Elise might be trying to break the ice here, hoping that Kaia will give her some insight into what Jason's thinking. About how he's feeling about the whole thing. Of course she's on edge, and Kaia would like to soothe her frazzled nerves if she can.

She wonders if she can do that without taking some of the wind out of Jason's sails, or betraying his confidence.

"I don't think you have anything to be embarrassed about. Wanting to protect the people we love makes us do some crazy things sometimes," she says, thinking back on the whole security detail debacle. Even though Jason still insists on keeping Paul and company around, just in case, it was an eye-opening exercise in learning the lengths to which Jason would go to hold on to someone he cares about.

It doesn't surprise her at all that he would've learned something like that from Elise.

"Yes, it can. Doesn't make it right, though."

Kaia nods. "I think it's easy to forgive someone for loving you so much that they'd be willing to do whatever it was they thought was right for you, no matter how difficult. Even though those things might change over time."

Elise takes a deep breath, and gives Kaia a genuine, if small, smile.

"I'm glad he found you, Kaia. There was a time when I didn't think he would."

"I'm glad he found me, too. He's a remarkable person, Elise. You should be proud to have raised such a man."

Her eyes sparkle with unshed tears. "I had a hand in it, at least. And thank you."

Elise holds out her hand, and gives it a squeeze.

"You about ready?" Jason asks, basically appearing in the doorway behind them out of nowhere. "Paul's waiting for you in the foyer."

"Where are you going?" Elise asks, as Kaia reluctantly puts

down her wine and stands up.

"Security guard Paul and I are going to be doing a little sightseeing this afternoon." What she doesn't say is, *so that you and Jason can have a little time alone.*

"I've given him a list of destinations. He's not to deviate from that list."

"You want to show me all the special places, huh?" Kaia asks, stepping up to give Jason a peck on the cheek.

He leans down and whispers in her ear. "You know how much I like showing you my special places."

Just out of earshot of his surrogate mother, but still enough to make her blush.

"I'll see you later," she says. "Maybe I'll bring you a tacky souvenir."

"I'm looking forward to it."

"Thank you for the wine, Elise."

With a gentle nod and a smile, Elise says, "Oh, honey, you're welcome. I think we'll be sharing more, soon enough."

Chapter 26

Jason takes the seat that Kaia just vacated, and finishes off the rest of her wine in three long gulps.

"Pace yourself," Elise warns. "You're a terrible wine drunk."

Jason laughs, which is something he hadn't imagined doing during this conversation when he'd thought about it. And he'd thought about it a lot over the past couple of weeks. Almost constantly during the flight over here.

"I am," he admits. "Of all the things you choose to remember about me."

Elise gives him a soft smile. "I remember everything about you, Jason. The day you said your first word, the day you lost your first tooth. Your first day of high school, your first date, your first hangover," she says, turning her head and giving him a pointed look. She sits up, and sets her glass down on the table between them. "You aren't my son, but…I've always loved you like you were."

Jason swallows past the lump that's in his throat. "I know you have." She took him in after his parents died. She could've sent him off to boarding school, or made him someone else's problem. But she always made him feel loved, and wanted. And she always tried to do right by him.

"I'm sorry about that night," she says, her voice wavering. "I'm sorry I kept the truth from you for as long as I did. I know it wound up doing more harm than good, but-"

"I didn't come with a manual, Elise. Seems to me that parenting is a learn-as-you go kind of thing. And you always told me that we never stop learning."

With a watery smile, Elise says, "No, we don't."

"I'm sorry for how I acted that night. I shouldn't have pushed you away like that, but I have a lifetime of dealing with things that way, and it takes a while to unlearn it. Not that that's an excuse; it isn't, I was just hurt and surprised. I was mad at Mom and Dad. I was mad at *you*. I was…confused. Angry, because I'd lived my life looking over my shoulder for so long when I didn't need to. I was scared of something that didn't even exist."

"I don't blame you, Jason. Not for any of those things. And I wouldn't blame you if you were still angry with me. I know it's going to take a while to earn back your trust-"

"I *do* trust you, Elise. You've given me a lifetime of reasons to do that. One screw-up isn't going to change that. Besides," he says, smiling at her. "I'm not even sure it was a screw up."

She raises her brow. "Why's that?"

"I've been thinking a lot about the course of my life, ever since that night. How different things might've been for me if I'd known the truth a little sooner. Kaia helped me understand why you kept it from me, why you wanted me to have a good memory of them. I know you'd never intentionally hurt me, so I can't hold your good intentions against you, especially not when that road led me straight to Kaia. Or maybe it led Kaia to me, I still haven't figured that one out."

Elise laughs. "Well, that's certainly one way of looking at it."

"It's the positive way," Jason explains. "I'm feeling more positive about my life lately."

"I can tell. It's a good look on you."

"You think?" Jason asks, pleased.

"I do. A man in love is a sight to behold."

Jason doesn't shy away from it. He doesn't even try to deflect. "I am in love with her."

"I couldn't have picked a better match for you myself. I'm…"

"You're what?"

"I don't want to push," she explains quickly. "But I'm very much hoping I see the two of you around here more often."

Jason has spent the better part of his adult life avoiding this place. He comes here when he needs to, and only when business requires it. The past was just too painful, and everywhere he looked he saw nothing but his parents, and felt nothing but sadness.

He thinks that in time, if he's willing to *take* that time, that he can start loving this city again. Especially if he rediscovers it through Kaia's eyes.

"I think you can count on that. I'm hoping Kaia would like to start spending more time here, too. New York is our home, but I think we might make this a more frequent destination."

Elise smiles. "I'm glad to hear that, Jason."

"C'mere," she says, standing, and brushing the wrinkles out of her dress. He does as she asks, and she pushes up on her tiptoes to wrap him up in a fierce hug.

"I love you, kid."

The words bring him peace, and he finds himself smiling. "I love you, too."

On a bench along the banks of the San Francisco Bay, Kaia cuddles up against Jason's side, searching for some warmth.

"I brought a blanket," he says, reaching into the bag at his feet, and pulling it out. He drapes it over her shivering body.

"You're wonderful. Amazing. Your foresight is one of the things I love most about you."

Jason laughs, then reaches back into the bag. "It's a good thing I brought this, then." He puts the still-warm thermos in her outstretched hands.

"Coffee?"

"Better. Hot chocolate."

Kaia lets out a high-pitched squeal of delight as she pulls off the top, and pours a little into the attached mug.

"I may or may not have spiked it."

"Mmm…" She presses a warm kiss to his cheek. "My hero."

She takes a sip, then offers the mug to him.

"No thanks," he says, wrapping his arm around her, holding on tight. "I'm driving, remember?"

"Trying to get me all liquored up, are you?"

Jason laughs. "Maybe just a little."

"You'd like me tipsy."

"I'm sure I'll love you tipsy."

"Tipsy me is a little bit looser. It's a shame you didn't bring a driver. We could've fooled around in the back seat while he drove us home."

Just a minute ago, she'd praised him for his foresight, and the thought hadn't even occurred to him at all. Now, he's regretting it. Still, "We can always fool around in the car before we head back."

"Ah, like a couple of horny teenagers. Sounds like a plan."

"I'm looking forward to it."

She pulls the blanket up around her neck, before she rests her head on his shoulder, her hair brushing his neck. She sighs, then looks up at the sky, streaked with the bright yellows and pinks of the setting sun.

"I love it here. It's so gorgeous."

"Yeah?"

"Mmm. I've never been to California before. I think you picked the perfect place to bring me for my first time."

He loves that she loves his hometown, and he wants to make her fall even more in love with it if that's possible.

"I've seen a lot of this state, and it's all really nice. But this? This city is the best."

"I think you're a little biased," she teases.

"Maybe a little."

"But I believe you."

Jason likes the sound of those words. He knows this is something totally trivial, but he never wants her to doubt him. Not ever.

"Like it enough to come back?"

She crooks her head in his direction, and gives him a thoughtful look. "Your talk with Elise went well, huh?"

"It did," he explains. "But that's not the only reason I want to come back."

"It's a good enough reason for me. But just for kicks, why don't you tell me the other one?"

"I always loved this place growing up, but there came a point in my life where I couldn't wait to leave. I was…I was running away from things. I'm not the kind of man who runs anymore. And I'd like to come back here more often, make this town and the people in it a part of my life again."

Kaia smiles up at him, like this is the best news she's heard in a while. "I think that's a great idea."

"It would be nice if you wanted that, too."

"What exactly are you asking me for, Jason?"

"I'm not asking you to uproot your life, Kaia. New York is home. What I am asking you for is long weekends here and there, if you're willing to give them."

It's too early, he knows this. But at some point, Jason is going to ask her for forever. Wherever in the world Kaia wants that to be.

"Would we come and stay with Elise, or-"

He only hesitates a moment before he says, "I was thinking I'd buy a place. A condo overlooking the bay, maybe? We can decide that later."

He doesn't miss the way she looks up at him when he says "we." He means it, too. He only wants to take this step if she takes it with him.

"Maybe, at some point, when you get a handle on your new clients, you could look into taking on some accounts out here. Go bicoastal. Expand."

If it wasn't for the small smile that was steadily growing, he'd be worried about her silence. He's more than happy to give her whatever time she needs to think about it, but he hopes she'll agree.

For a long while, they both sit there together, watching the sunset as the waves lap against the sand in the background. Even though Jason's whole future is basically hanging in the air between them, he's at peace.

Then, Kaia finally says, "It sounds nice."

Jason laughs, then says, "Which part?"

"All of it. The condo, expanding my business…the long weekends, you and me together. For as long as you want it."

He's going to want it all forever, he knows.

For now, it's enough.

Chapter 27

Jason sits on the edge of the bed, nervously watching Kaia packing her suitcase. He tries to hide it, sure, but she can read him like a book.

"You need to unclench," she teases, winking at him as she walks into their closet.

"Easy for you to say," she hears him yell from the bedroom. "I'm not the one going to Vegas for a bachelorette party."

Kaia peers out of the doorway at her husband-to-be, looking adorably on edge. "Do you *want* to go to Vegas for a bachelorette party?"

Jason rolls his eyes. "You know what I mean."

"What I know is that I've explained this to you about a thousand times."

He reaches out for her, taking her hand in his and pulling her closer, and the way he looks at her is completely unfair.

He's too handsome for his own good. He's too handsome for *her* own good.

"Explain it to me a thousand and one times, then."

Kaia sighs, then leans down and kisses Jason's beautiful, pouty mouth.

"We're just going out for a little girl time before the wedding. No bachelorette party, no strippers."

He pulls a face at the word, but Kaia continues.

"We're just going to drink, gossip, and get mani-pedis by the pool. The upside is that I'll have a really nice tan for our honeymoon."

That gets a grin out of him. "Good, because I don't think we're going to be spending much time outside." He moves in and sucks a quick kiss on her neck, making her shiver.

"Not fair, you're playing dirty."

He hums against her skin. "My favorite way to play."

"You're not going to distract me today. The plane is leaving soon."

"It's my jet. It can take off whenever."

"*Jason*," she pleads.

With a groan, he lets her go.

"It's just three days," she assures him.

"Three *long* days."

She can't argue with him there.

"When I come back, we're getting married, Jason. Then you'll have a whole lifetime of me." She zips her suitcase, and places it on the floor next to the bed. Jason looks at it like it's personally offending him. "At some point during our marriage, you'll probably wish I was away for three long days."

"Never," he says with conviction, his eyes full of fiery passion.

"Ugh, don't look at me like that."

"Like what?"

"Like *that*," Kaia replies, pointing at Jason's stupidly handsome face. "Like I hung the moon, and you want to devour me. It's very inconvenient when I'm trying to make a point."

"I'll be happy to make things more inconvenient for you," he says lasciviously.

She hates herself a little for wanting to stay. Maybe she can push the flight back an hour, hour and a half...no. *No.*

"I'm leaving now."

Jason's head lolls back in exasperation. "Fine. Come here and give me a kiss."

That's one request that she absolutely cannot resist.

"It's one of my last ones as a single woman," she teases. "Make it count."

Jason reaches up, slides his fingers through her hair, and *oh*. He makes it *count*. When they both finally come up for air, Kaia's more than a little dazed, and Jason looks triumphant.

With shaky hands, she grabs the handle of her suitcase, and wheels it to the bedroom door. "I'll see you on Saturday. I'll be the one in the dress at the end of the aisle."

He grins. "I'll make sure I'm on time."

"It's a date then," she tells him.

With a wink, he replies, "Sure is."

Kaia smiles at the man she's going to spend the rest of her life with. Forever's never been so beautiful.

About The Author

Cassie Cross is a Maryland native and a romantic at heart, who lives outside of Baltimore with her two dogs and a closet full of shoes. Cassie's fondness for swoon-worthy men and strong women are the inspiration for most of her stories, and when she's not busy writing a book, you'll probably find her eating takeout and indulging in her love of 80's sitcoms.

Cassie loves hearing from her readers, so please follow her on Twitter (@ CrossWrites) or leave a review for this book on the site you purchased it from. Thank you!

Printed in Great Britain
by Amazon